D1407960

Can You Sue
Your Parents For
Malpractice?

Also by Paula Danziger

THE CAT ATE MY GYMSUIT

THE PISTACHIO PRESCRIPTION

7878

Can You Sue Your Parents For Malpractice?

A NOVEL BY

Paula Danziger

Delacorte Press

LIBRARY
NORTHEASTERN JUNIOR HIGH

11357 1/90 14.95

Published by
Delacorte Press
Bantam Doubleday Dell Publishing Group, Inc.
666 Fifth Avenue
New York, New York 10103

Copyright © 1979 by Paula Danziger

All rights reserved. No part of this book may be
reproduced or transmitted in any form or by any means,
electronic or mechanical, including photocopying,
recording or by any information storage and retrieval
system, without the written permission of the Publisher,
except where permitted by law.

Manufactured in the United States of America

9

Library of Congress Cataloging in Publication Data

Danziger, Paula, 1944–
    Can you sue your parents for malpractice?

    SUMMARY: Confused about her life at home and at
school, 14-year-old Lauren learns the importance of being
her own person.
    [1.   Family problems—Fiction.   2.   Individuality—
Fiction]   I.   Title.
PZ7.D2394Cam   [Fic]   78-72856
ISBN 0-385-28112-9
MV

When I teach people, I marry them.
SYLVIA ASHTON WARNER, *Teacher*

Some days I wanted a divorce.
PAULA DANZIGER

This book is dedicated to all my students, ever, especially: Lincoln Junior High School, West Orange, N.J. 1977–78

PERIOD 2—Wes Arlein, Jamie Batterman, Marc Begun, Michael Bruno, Renée Feldman, Beverly Fong, Andrew Gaynor, Steven Gerber, Ellen Gordon, Jon Herbst, Traci Husid, Tom Ippolito, Stephen Judd*, Laura Juliano*, Heidi Ladell*, Cathy Lee, Lynne Lenkowsky, Maureen Mason, Scott Nelson, Ilyse Odesky, Patti Russo, Andi Sable*, Michelle Skarbnik, Mitchell Sussis

(cont'd)

*Also on *The Log*

PERIOD 3—Journalism: *The Lincoln Log*—Linda Baker, Julie Bossie, Laura Fajvan, Elyssa Kolin, Wendy Juliano, David Manspeizer, Vincent Pallito, Abby Sarret, Jay Scharer, Eric Schondorf, Jeanne Senney, Marvin Silverman, Marla Zimring

PERIOD 4—Gail Broad, Judy Bromberg*, Michelle Butensky*, Mark Davis, Ilene Davison, Mitchell Gervis, Linda Grossman, Angie Jones, Adam Kaletsky, Monica Kaszerman*, Bill Kievning, Wendy Kolton*, Laurie Kopp*, Gail Levine, Donna Molinaro, Nancy Nolan*, Pat Phalen, Mike Pitch, Bonnie Quinn, Max Silverman, Dale Sippel, Lauren Weiss

PERIOD 5—Raymond Beck, Scott Cabe, Danny Distasio, Dianne Hendriksen, Danny J. Kaylor, Kara Luisi, Elaine Mijailidis, Michael Neglio, Jean O'Neil, Sam Rockaway, Todd Ruja, Paul Slivka, Andy Tulli

PERIOD 7—Maria Armenti, Debbie Calimano, Tom Commandeur, Donny Dalgauer, Ronnie DeAngleus, Patti Dugan, George Falus, Pete Feinblatt, Jackie Geswelli, Chuck Helfeld, Jill Henning, Lee Herman, Liz Holstein, Mark Kelly, Lisa Kuhlmann, Michael Parlin, Ed Pringle, Bonnie Raskind, Lisa Renna, Lee Sherwood, Andrea Weisbard, Paula Whittington, Joan Zink

ALSO—Betsy Gaynor, Joci Krasner, Mark Licht, Anthony Picillo, Tommy Popple, Leslie Schwartz, Rusty Wagner, Andy Weinstein, Ian Ziering

And to the memory of His Principalship, O. Stanley Stonesifer, a truly fine educator and human being.

Chapter 1

"Lauren, why was the skeleton afraid to cross the road?"

I pretend I don't hear Linda.

She keeps talking anyway. "Because he had no guts."

It's hard coping with a ten-year-old sister who wants to be a stand-up comic and treats the family as a captive audience for all her routines. It's especially hard while I'm trying to get over a broken heart.

"Look," I say, "would you please go away? I've got to study my Spanish. There's a quiz tomorrow. I flunked the last one and I've got to get an A on this one, or else."

"Just one more. Please, Lauren, then I promise to go."

I wonder how many other fourteen-year-olds in the world have to deal with a younger sister determined to take her show on the road. It's not that

I don't like her, it's just that my mind's on other things right now.

She looks so hurt.

I say, "Oh, OK. But just one more. I really do have to study. You'll see what it's like when you get to ninth grade and have to worry about grades to get into college."

She grins. "Did you hear the one about the rodent who almost drowned and his brother had to give him mouse to mouse resuscitation?"

"Out," I yell. "Enough is enough."

Linda goes, "Da da di da da da," and tap dances out of the room.

I laugh at the dumb joke after she leaves, and shake my head. She's got a right to her dreams. It's just that my mind's on other things right now.

My special elective class, "Law for Children and Young People," is about to start. And I definitely have lots of questions. It's a good thing the school started it just in time for everything I have to ask. The first one's going to be "What are the grounds for justifiable homicide?" Can I kill off one or more of the following: an older sister who gets her own room and ends up with all the beauty genes in the family? A mother who lives in a fantasy world always dreaming about winning the lottery or some big prize so we can all live happily ever after? A mother who's always writing letters and going to tryouts for quiz shows? A father who constantly complains about how hard it is to sell insurance and to support a family in this day and age? Sandy Linwood, who stole my boyfriend because she goes further than I do?

It's absolutely disgusting being fourteen. You've got no rights whatsoever. Your parents get to make all the decisions: Who gets the single bedroom. How much allowance is enough. What time you must come in. Who is a proper friend. What your report card is supposed to look like. And what your parents don't tell you to do, the school does. What section you're in. What's good literature. What courses you have to take to fulfill their requirements. The worst thing is that the more I realize what I want to do, the stricter everyone becomes.

The school started all sorts of new electives this year, based on what teachers want to teach and what they think we want. Last year no one wanted to run for PTA president and when Ms. Corday finally said she'd run, everyone voted for her because she was the only one. She's turned out to be radical, which is great for the kids, since she wants all new things tried out. And the school's always trying to please the PTA, so we got some great things. One of them is "Law for Children and Young People." It's so popular they had to put all the names of students who wanted it into a bowl and pick out thirty names. I got chosen, which is lucky because it's my only chance before I graduate and go over to the high school. And since I've decided to become a lawyer, it's very important to me.

I guess the big tragedy in my life, at the moment, is that Bobby Taylor jilted me for Sandy Linwood. It's hard to lose your first real boyfriend because he wants to do more than you do. Just because he's two years older than I am he said things like what a real child I am, a late bloomer. Can I help it if I've been taught that virginity's important? Can I help it if Bobby prefers Sandy, who probably has "Lust Is a Must" and "Chaste Makes Waste" as mottos? She's a cheerleader. They ought to have rules against cheerleaders doing that sort of stuff. It would serve her right if she had to turn in her pom-poms and megaphone. I just hope that they both get some terrible disease and rot away. It's going to be really hard to ever trust a man again. There's not much chance that I'm ever going to get involved again. It hurts too much. Anyway, there's no one else I'm interested in.

There's a knock on the bedroom door.

"Lauren, OK if I come in?"

"Sure," I yell. Melissa's not so bad for an older sister except that she gets everything, like her own room and no curfews and clothes before they become hand-me-downs. She's also my father's favorite, although he'd deny it and say he cares about all of us equally.

She floats in. Other people walk; not Melissa. She's got a special style.

She sits down on Linda's bed and says, "Think I could borrow your lumber jacket? I'm going to a concert tonight at the college and they're holding it outside in the amphitheater."

Remembering the plaid poncho she lent me for my first date with Bobby, I say, "Sure."

She says, "Thanks," and starts brushing her hair.

"Melissa, when you go out with Mike, how far do you go?" I ask, trying to sound nonchalant.

"What?" She drops her brush on the floor and looks for it under the bed.

"I said, how far do you and Mike go?" I think that for someone who is nineteen, she's losing her hearing awfully quickly.

"Lauren Allen, that's really none of your business. Do I ever ask how far you go with any of the pimple-faced kids you hang out with?"

Hang out is right. That's all it ever was 'til Bobby. And then it wasn't much. At least he didn't think so. Personally I think men should be willing to love women for their poetic qualities. And I think the comment about pimples isn't very nice. Ms. Clear Skin shouldn't make fun of people who have a few zits. The only guy I've ever known with skin problems that were major was John Hiller, and he went to the dermatologist and looks fine now.

"When I was your age," Melissa goes on, "I never asked anyone how far they went. So you're just going to have to keep wondering. I have a right to my own life." She sticks out her tongue at me.

I never give up that easily. Future lawyers have to be relentless in their questioning. And even though I've sworn off men, I can always use any information to store away in case I have to defend some women in court cases concerning males. "All those times you say you're staying with Cindy in the dorm, do you really? Come on, you can tell me. I won't be a stoolie."

She laughs. "Cut it out. Ever since you were a baby, you've asked a million questions. You're impossible."

"How else am I supposed to learn?"

"Don't they teach you anything in health class?" She's still brushing her long hair.

"Sure they do." I think about Miss Crawford, not Ms., Miss Crawford, who's about ninety-two and tells us that if we're going to sit on a boy's lap, we should put a telephone book on it first. "But I'd rather hear it from someone who's had field experience, not from someone who says, 'It's a wife's duty.' "

"Crawford always was warped, but she's got tenure and they can't do anything about her," Melissa says. "Lauren, why don't you do your own fieldwork? Does this have something to do with the breakup with Bobby? Do you want to talk about it?"

It's just too embarrassing, so I say, "OK, you win. Let's change the subject." Sometimes I'm sorry that my best friend, Bonnie, ever fixed me up on a blind date with him.

Melissa puts down the hairbrush. "Are you sure? I know it's impossible to get Mom to talk about sex. With three daughters, you'd think she'd be able to say more than 'We'll discuss this when you decide to get married. Just don't do anything before then.'"

I smile. "That's the line I got when I tried to ask her a question when I was a little kid. Then she told me about the birds and bees. I wanted to hear about humans."

Melissa giggles and puts down her hairbrush. "It's hard at your age. I guess it's always hard, but I think junior high's the worst. It was for me. So if you want to talk, just let me know."

I think about how mad I get at her for getting her own room, more privileges, and more new clothes, and then feel guilty when I see how nice she can be.

I change the subject. It's difficult sharing real feelings with anyone. "My elective begins on Monday. I'm so excited. I got the law course I wanted."

"Matthews is teaching it, right?" she asks.

I nod.

"He's just gorgeous. Practically every female I know had a crush on him when he arrived. I never did get his history class, though. Just used to drool every time I saw him in the hall. You're going to love him."

Fat chance. Men have no place in my life. I've loved and lost and will never love again. The hurt is too much to bear. It just isn't worth it. "Not me. I just plan to learn as much law as I can."

"We'll see." She grins.

I ignore her know-it-all attitude and change the subject. "Where's everyone?"

She says, "Mom and Dad went over to Sears to price a new washing machine."

Thank goodness. When the washing machine broke down and the repairperson told my parents to hold funeral services for it, I was afraid we'd have to do our clothes with a washboard and tub, like in the pioneer times. I was afraid it was going to be like the dishwasher. After Linda accidentally put the liquid detergent in the dishwasher, instead of the regular stuff, and it foamed all over the kitchen, our parents decided it was too expensive to fix. Now we have to take turns with the dishes.

"You and I are here," she says. "That's four so far. And Linda's telling jokes to Gopher."

Now that's a captive audience. My weirdo sister's telling jokes to a dog who's tied up in the cellar due to an unfortunate encounter with a skunk— who won.

She looks around the room. "I can't believe how you and Linda have such different taste. This room looks like it's been split down the middle. Couldn't you have at least agreed on the same bedspreads?"

I look at the room. She's absolutely right but I wanted the bright-orange bedspread and Linda wanted a plaid one and neither of us would give in. So Mom decided to let us each decorate our own side of the room the way we wanted.

"And doesn't it drive you nuts, being such a neat person with Linda such a slob?"

There are books all over the floor on Linda's side . . . and stuffed animals on the floor and clothes on her bed.

"Some people," I say, "are lucky and don't have to share their room with anyone else so they can develop their own sense of style. And do you have any idea what it's like to be in the ninth grade and have to share a room with someone whose idea of a good time is pretending that her Ken doll is taking her Barbie doll out for pizza?"

She keeps brushing her hair. I watch and am jealous of her long frosted hair. My mother says

I can't bleach my hair until college. Doomed to a high-school life of turd-brown curls that won't be controlled. And freckles to match. Gross.

"Look, I'm sorry I mentioned it. If I had my choice, you know I'd move into the dorm immediately and you could take my room. But, as we are told constantly, Dad can't afford it and he makes too much for me to get financial aid, so I'm stuck commuting to a state college while all my friends get to go out of state. Think I'm happy about that?"

I stand up on the bed. "Well, I'm going to law school. He's had to pay for braces for you and they're going to get them for Linda. He should put the money he saved on my straight teeth into a special college fund just for me so that someday I can be super lawyer." I jump up and down on my bed. "I plan to preserve truth and justice and the democratic process—to help the poor, the maltreated, the innocent." Then I do a forward flip on the bed and land on my back.

She laughs. "You're crazy, but then that seems to run in this family. I think I'm the only sane one."

Sane. Sure. I consider reminding her of the time people asked her to run for homecoming queen of the high school. She said no and then tried to get a write-in campaign to make Gopher the queen. Her slogan was: "Elect a real dog. Beauty is only skin deep and these contests are sexist, anyway." Mary Anne Lothrop beat Gopher out by only about ten points. And Melissa thinks she's cornered the market on family sanity.

I stare at the ceiling. "Why couldn't we have been born rich instead of middle class?"

"It could have been worse. But that would be nice. Then Mom wouldn't always be dreaming of winning prizes. If only Dad didn't think it's awful for women with a family to work, then maybe she could go to work and not be so bored."

Gopher bounds in and jumps on my bed. I guess he had to escape from listening to Linda's monologues, or someone took pity and untied him. The dumb mutt smells like a combination of Eau de Skunk and tomato juice. He starts to lick my face. Grossness.

Melissa holds her nose and says, "Mike's picking me up in a few minutes. OK if I take the jacket out of the closet?"

"Sure." I fend off Gopher with a pillow.

She gets up to leave. "And if you ever want to talk about what happened between you and Bobby, maybe I can help."

"Not unless you want to be an accomplice to the murder of a sixteen-year-old creep," I say, trying to sit up with our monster of a German shepherd jumping all over me.

She shakes her head.

I watch her leave and start to say something. Gopher licks me in the mouth. Yeech!

I lie down on my bed and stare at the ceiling again. When the new elective starts, I'm going to find out if it's possible to sue Sandy Linwood for alienation of affection.

Chapter 2

The weekend at last.

Linda and I are alone in the kitchen. My parents, after much discussion and comparison shopping, have gone back to Sears to buy the washing machine.

My turn to clear the table and wash the breakfast dishes. Linda dries and puts away. Only she's too short, so I end up putting the stuff into the cabinets. Life just isn't fair. Everyone should have equal responsibility. But no. Melissa's out. Dad says that as breadwinner, his job is finished once the groceries are paid for. Mom says that once the meal is cooked and on the table, she's done. It's just not fair. Fourteen and fated to a life of dishpan hands. I wish Linda had never messed up the dishwasher. So does she, now that we're stuck with this job. I tried to explain to Mom, but all she did was go out and buy a new detergent supposed to keep hands youthful. How kind, how thoughtful. What ever happened to child labor laws? Minimum wage? That's why I'm going to become a lawyer to see that kids get an even break.

"Lauren?" Linda says.

"Yes?" I wonder why people don't just keep talking once they've said the name.

"Did you hear the one about the guy who only works on Saturdays and Sundays because he's a candle trimmer and they only work on wick ends?"

"Linda, cut that one from your act. That's awful," I say, trying to get a glass clean.

She smiles and dries a saucer.

"Lauren."

"Not another one. Please, I can't take it."

"No, this time I want to ask you something." She blows a very large bubble. She can do that because she always puts the whole pack in her mouth at once.

I'm tempted to smash it all over her face. Not to be mean. Just because it's there.

"This is important to me," she says.

There's bubble gum on her lips from where she's popped it inward.

She stays quiet for a few minutes and then very softly she asks, "How old were you when you stopped wearing an undershirt?"

I want to laugh, but I remember how wearing an undershirt was once the grossest thing in the world for me. So I say, "For my eleventh birthday, Mom bought me a training bra."

She giggles. "Like a training bicycle, with wheels for extra support?"

I can't help laughing now. "Kind of. Keeps you on balance, psychologically. Listen, why don't you talk to Mom, tell her you want a bra?"

"I did. She said to wait 'til something starts happening or until I'm eleven, whichever comes first. But that's not for nine whole months and Judy's mother just bought her one."

It's tough when your friends start developing first, even though I remember how weird my friend Bonnie felt when she was the first one in the class to wear a bra. I guess there's no way of winning. "Don't worry. It'll happen to you."

"Every day I check under my arms to see if hair's growing. Nothing. I'm probably going to be in the Guinness Book of Records. Latest developer in the world." She looks absolutely miserable.

I want to hug her but my hands are covered with dish suds. "Lin, honey, you know what? I bet I still have my training bra someplace. I was going to bronze it like Mom did with our baby shoes but I decided that they probably wouldn't bronze padding. After we get done here, we'll go look for it."

"You're the best sister in the whole world!"

I look at her and wonder if she'll remember that

the next time we have a fight about the room. Being a sister is not always the easiest thing in the world, but sometimes it's pretty good. Especially when you know it's so hard to trust people in the outside world. Especially heartbreakers.

She's smiling. "Lauren, do you know what the best medicine is for a pig with a sprained ankle?"

Oh, no. The kid never lets up.

"Oinkment. And when is a pig like ink?" she asks. "When it's in the pen," she answers herself, and then takes a bow even though no one's clapping.

I accidentally drop the Brillo pad into the soapy water and have to find it, so I can ignore her.

"How can you tell there's been an elephant in your refrigerator?"

"By the footprints on the Jell-O," I say. "Linda, come on. Cut it out."

She dries a glass. "What's yellow, has four wheels, and lies on its back?"

She's got me on that one.

"A dead school bus."

"My turn. Whose initials are L.A. and will not be given my training bra if she doesn't quit driving me nuts?"

"Don't you think I'm funny?" she asks.

I think about it. "Sometimes. But sometimes it gets on my nerves."

"Oh, OK. But I have to practice. What am I going to do if some big entertainer gets sick and they need a last-minute replacement?"

"How are they going to know to call you?"

She smiles. "I wrote to all the big nightclubs and television shows telling them I'm available."

It really must run in our family. My mother's always writing letters, asking to be put on some big quiz show, and they always write back and tell her that she's on a long waiting list.

"We'll worry about that later. Now let's finish up and go look for the training bra. Then Bonnie and I are going shopping."

While we're finishing up, I think about Bobby and how much he hurt me. I wish there were a novocaine to numb my heart. That's why I'm never going to love again. You get hurt and don't get over it. I'm glad that I learned this in the ninth grade so that I won't ever go through it again. I'll just devote myself to law. I just hope that someday Bobby realizes what he gave up. I may not be that great, but Sandy's no bargain. It takes all her brain power just to remember the cheers and cartwheel at the same time.

We go upstairs.

I look in my mirror. Five feet four inches. Same long dull brown frizzy hair. Greenish-blue eyes. Probably the best thing about me. Freckles. Too many of them. An OK body, could probably lose about five pounds.

I think about what Linda's going through at her age and what she's got ahead. Maybe she'll be lucky like Melissa: able to get over heartbreaks and go out and find someone as nice as Mike. Maybe she'll be like me and never get over it. It's a rough road ahead.

I turn to Linda and say, "Come on, Munchkin. Let's look for the bra. I think it's in a shoe box."

That's where we find it, under my bed. With only one closet for two people, there's never enough room. The shoe box has the bra, a dried-out corsage from my eighth-grade dance, a broken guitar string rumored to have once been used by a Beatle, and a six-foot-long chain made up of Juicy Fruit wrappers.

Linda jumps up and down, grabs the bra out of my hands, and rushes into the closet, shutting the door behind her.

"What are you doing?" I yell. "You've never gotten dressed in a closet before."

Her muffled voice comes through the closet door: "Yeah, but I never had to put on a bra. It's different with undershirts."

She emerges holding her T-shirt in front of her from the waist up.

"Come on. Let's see," I say.

She blushes and drops the shirt.

I loosen the straps so that the bra's not so close to her chin.

"It's fine," I say.

She puts her T-shirt back on. "Are you sure?"

"Look in the mirror. See for yourself."

She throws back her shoulders and looks at the mirror. There's a grin on her face. "I have to call Judy to tell her I got a bra, too. Thanks. I just hope she doesn't get her period first."

She starts to walk out the door.

We can hear my mother coming up the steps, yelling, "We're home. Where is everyone?"

Linda throws herself on the bed, chest down.

My mother comes in. "Well, we got one. At the price of washing machines, I'm not sure gold wouldn't be cheaper. I just wish I had gotten on a quiz show so we wouldn't have had to spend all that money ourselves."

She starts to straighten up the clothes on Linda's side of the room. "Come on, Lin, get up and give me a hand."

"Can't I just lie here for a few minutes? You don't have to do that, Mom. I'll do it when you go downstairs."

At first I can't figure out what the problem is. Then I catch on. The training bra. Mom said no and Linda got one anyway. I wonder if I'm going to be in trouble, the party of the second part, helping the party of the first part, or something like that. I wonder whether giving her the bra is legal. Oh well, it's important to her.

My mother says, "Get up, now. What's going on?"

"Look, Mom, I'll help her clean up. You don't have to."

"Now I know something's going on here. A mother always knows. Lauren, you never offer to help her clean up. You just complain about it."

Linda sits up, with her shoulders rounded.

"So that's it. Do you have a bra on? Did you get it from Lauren or buy it while we were out? You know I told you to wait."

Linda starts to cry. "But everyone in the whole world has one but me . . . and Michelle Haley."

Michelle Haley lives next to us and is six years old. I think Linda's carrying this a little too far.

My mother walks over to her and says, "Stand up straight, Linda Allen."

Linda does.

"Well," my mother says, "I don't like the fact that you disobeyed me, but I guess this is very important to you, so all right. But I don't like it. You don't need it, first of all. And second, I guess I don't like to see my baby growing up."

"It's OK, Mom. I'm still not all grown up."

My mother sighs. "I feel like I always stay the same but my girls are constantly changing. You wearing a bra. Melissa's stopped wearing one. I guess that's part of the deal when you're a mother. At least it is for me."

I think of my friends' mothers and how that's true for some of them and different for others.

"And what about you, Lauren? Is there anything new that I should know about you?" she asks.

I shake my head.

She says, "Would you girls like to do something after lunch? Your father's watching the football game on TV. How about going shopping with me, to the supermarket?"

"Sorry, I've already promised Bonnie I'd go to the shopping center with her," I say.

"I'll go with you, Mom," Linda says. "But first let me call Judy."

My mother nods and heads for the door. "I'll meet you downstairs."

As she leaves, Linda says, "I guess she's not as mad as I thought she would be. At least she didn't kill me. Do you think Dad will?"

I think back. "No, he'll just pretend he doesn't notice. That's what he did with Melissa and me."

She giggles. "Then I guess I made it. Wait 'til I tell Judy."

She goes out to make her phone call.

I lie down on my bed and think about how important all that used to be. Sometimes I wonder if there's ever going to be a time when there aren't things to worry about.

Chapter 3

Allowance. Saturday ritual. My father hands it to me as if he were giving away a million dollars.

I have to interrupt his precious football game to ask him for it.

He's sitting in his chair, the chair in which no one else can sit when he's around. He's drinking a can of beer, eating a hamburger, and watching two teams of grown men carrying a stupid ball, trying to break each other's bodies. I hate it. It's so awful. And Sandy Linwood cheers for stuff like that.

"What do you want, Lauren? Can't you see that I'm busy?"

"I just want my allowance. Please." I feel as if I have to beg for it, even though I do work around the house. Maybe I should do what Beverly Wells does, get a paper route. Then I won't have to ask him for the money. But I'd still have to help around the house. And if I had a paper route and it rained, I'd have to be outside and my hair would get even frizzier. So I guess there's just no way out.

I'm lucky. He's into the game, so he just says, "Don't spend it foolishly. You know how hard it is for me to earn it and to keep this family going."

I'm very lucky. Usually I get a much longer lecture, about how prices are inflated, how high the family dental bills are, how ungrateful children are.

I take the money and say, "Thanks."

He turns back to the game.

With this money and the rest that I've saved up, Bonnie and I can go ahead with our plan.

I grab some lunch, go back upstairs and call her. "Hi, it's me. All set?"

She says, "Sure."

I say, "Are you sure you want to go through with this? My parents are going to kill me when they see it. And you know how I hate the sight of blood."

"Don't weasel out of this one. Don't even try," she says. "You promised. We've talked about this for years."

"But what if I faint?"

"Look, you're only going to get your ears pierced, not have your appendix taken out." She laughs.

"But your mother won't kill you. My father once said he thought it was a barbaric practice. And I know he'll kill me for spending the money."

She sighs. "Well, if you don't want to get it done at the jeweler's, Marla said she'd do it for us. She did Andrea's and the holes are only a little lopsided."

The thought of a needle and an ice cube are more than I can bear. I give in. "We'll go to the jeweler's. You only live once."

"How soon can you get over here?" she wants to know.

"Ten minutes."

"See you then and, Lauren, don't worry. If you faint, I'll pick you up."

I go into my bedroom and look at myself in the mirror. I stare at my naked earlobes for the last time. Then I think of Jill Renna, who has two sets of holes and has lived to tell about it.

I think of all the excuses I can give my father. That it'll be cheaper because then I won't lose earrings anymore. That Bonnie gave it to me as an early birthday present and I gave it to her as a late birthday present. Maybe that'll work.

I sneak out of the house. No need to, but it'll be good practice for sneaking back in with my pierced earlobes.

My father's still got the television on. As I close

the door, he yells, "Don't slam it. Do you think you live in a barn?"

By the time I get to Bonnie's, I know I'm going to be the first person in history to die of complications caused by ear piercing.

Ms. Alda's at the door, in her tennis outfit and her fur coat. Bonnie's mother definitely has a style of her own. She's also got a license plate with her name on it.

"Have fun with your ear piercing, Lauren." She grins.

"Thanks, and have a nice time," I yell as she gets into her Mercedes.

She waves and drives off.

Even though Bonnie's my best friend, I get jealous sometimes because she's got so much money. I happen to live in the poorer section of the rich side of town. Some days, it seems like everyone has more than I do. People get to go on these great vacations and I just bet no one else gets as much grief as I do about how much I spend. I wonder if Melissa ever felt as strongly about it as I do, but I hate to ask her. She feels bad enough about having to go to a state college. She thinks that most state colleges rot.

Bonnie comes to the door. She's carrying her favorite stuffed animal, Moose. Moose was given to her by an old boyfriend. While she can't stand the guy anymore, she still has this thing for Moose. Being an only child does that to people sometimes.

"Hi, you ready?" I say, secretly hoping that since our phone call, she's contracted some minor disease that will keep her from leaving the house.

"In a minute. Just have to put on my boots." She pushes her bangs out of her face.

I come inside.

She yells from her room, "Come on in. Follow me."

I do and sit down on her bed. It's a giant room, with two closets. All for one person. I always want to ask if she'll trade Moose for one of my sisters, but somehow I don't think she would.

I lie down on her bed and watch as she puts on her boots. "Do you think it's going to hurt much? You know how I am about needles."

"We've been through this before. They use a machine like a hole puncher. It's real fast. Everyone says you don't feel a thing. You've just got to remember to keep using the peroxide so that it doesn't get infected. It's a breeze."

I stare at her ceiling. It's so high, and I love the mobile hanging from it.

"OK, ready or not, here we go." She's putting on her coat.

I debate throwing myself on her mercy and begging that we just go to a movie instead, but decide against it. I really do want to have my ears pierced. And the worst thing that can happen is that my parents will kill me. I guess I can live through that.

I get off the bed and start out the door with Bonnie.

We catch a bus to the shopping center.

The mall is an absolute zoo of people. It's almost impossible to get through the crowd even without the craft fair that's going on in the middle of everything. I stop at a table with handcrafted jewelry and think about how soon I'll be able to wear all the earrings that I like—the unusual kind. Well, not all, because they're not cheap, but some of them.

"Come on." Bonnie grabs my hand and pulls me to the front of the jewelry store.

I stare at all the stuff in the window, trying to stall for time.

She pulls me inside.

Maybe I should faint before I get it done. That way they can do it while I'm unconscious.

We go into the store.

"May I help you, girls?"

"We're here to get our ears pierced," Bonnie says.

The woman nods. "We do free ear piercing, as long as you purchase a set of gold earrings. They're over here." She leads us to a counter.

So many to choose from. They're beautiful. I just

hope that the ones I choose aren't much more than ten dollars or I'll have to spend my milk money for the week.

Bonnie picks out a pair of plain, small gold balls.

I pick out ones that the lady says are Florentine and cost ten dollars, plus tax. So far so good.

Then she takes us to the man behind the counter and tells him that we're going to have our ears pierced.

He takes us to a room in the back of the store. There's a door, a back exit. I guess that's where they take the bodies when they make mistakes.

"Now, who wants to go first?" he asks.

I step forward. I've got to get it over with before I have a heart attack.

He sits me down on a stool. I close my eyes and try to think of pleasant things, like school being called off because of snow.

He makes me open up my eyes so I can check to see if he's putting the hole where I want it.

I nod and look at the thing he's got in his hand. It does look like a hole puncher, only with a spike in it.

I close my eyes again and count to ten. I feel the thing go in and then I say, "Is it over?"

He hums and says, "The earring's even in. Now that wasn't so bad, was it?" and does the other side.

A snap. I get up and Bonnie walks slowly over and sits down on the stool.

I'm so busy looking at my ears that I don't even watch him do hers. At least not until I hear him say, "Put your head between your legs and sit there for a while. The dizziness will go away in a few minutes."

I turn around and see that Bonnie's incredibly pale. I walk over to her and hold on to her shoulders. "Are you OK?"

She says, "Just a little dizzy."

The man comes over and breaks something in front of her and puts it by her nose. "Smelling salts. You'll be all right in no time. I haven't lost a customer yet."

Bonnie's head comes up quickly. "Wow. Yeech! I'm OK now. No more of that."

We pay for the earrings and walk out of the store.

"Lauren," she says, "if you ever tell anyone that I almost passed out, I'm going to kill you."

"I promise. But don't forget how you made fun of me for being scared."

She giggles and apologizes.

I keep staring into store windows, trying to get my reflection so that I can see the earrings.

As we're about to go into a coffee shop for soda, this guy comes up to her. It's the new kid I've seen in the halls.

"Hi, Bonnie. How are you?"

"Oh, hi, Zack. Fine. And you?"

He nods and looks at me. He's got a wonderful smile.

Bonnie says, "Zack, this is my friend, Lauren Allen. Lauren, Zack Davids. His mother and mine went to high school together. He just moved here from California at the end of last marking period."

I say, "Nice to meet you. I've seen you in the halls."

Zack says, "I already know who you are."

Before I have a chance to ask how, Bonnie says, "We just got our ears pierced. Do you like them?"

What a spot to put him in. Why does she always do stuff like that?

He looks at our ears and says, "Fantastic. I really like the blood that's gushing down your left earlobe, Bonnie."

Quickly she opens her purse and pulls out a mirror.

"Got ya," Zack says.

He and I both laugh.

He's very cute. He's got sandy brown hair, dimples, great cheekbones. I'm an absolute nut about cheekbones. Bobby has great cheekbones. Bobby. Men. I remember my vow never to be interested in one again and look away.

"Well," Zack says, "I've got to run an errand for my mother. Lauren, it was nice meeting you in person." He takes off.

I say, "Bonnie, do you think he's seen me in the halls? Is that what he means?"

She shrugs. "I don't know. He's awfully nice, though. Our mothers had us meet one day when he first moved here. He's only in eighth grade though, so I didn't want to hang around with him."

In our school, it's living death for a ninth-grade girl to be seen with an eighth-grade guy. People just don't do it.

We go in and have a soda.

Bonnie continues to talk. "His older brother's away at college. Zack and his mother moved here after his parents got a divorce. My mother and Ms. Davids were once real close. They've become friends again. Since they're both divorced, they go to some of the same places."

Divorce. It seems like everyone I know has parents who have split up. Some kids even have a real father and a couple of stepfathers. And one mother and a couple of stepmothers. Melissa says it's like some kind of suburban virus and that she wants to make sure it never happens to her. I guess even though things aren't always wonderful at home, at least it's good my parents stay together and try to work it out.

Bonnie says, "Hey, you seem a million miles away. What are you thinking about?"

"I don't know. Divorce. Cheekbones."

She laughs. "You and those cheekbones. Zack does have a nice face, doesn't he. He's cute. An eighth grader, but cute. Look, Lauren, aren't you over Bobby yet? Why don't I fix you up with someone again? Dave's got a lot of nice friends."

Yeah. And Bobby's one of them. Ever since Bonnie and Dave have been going out, she's been after me to go out with his friends so we can double. Well, I did it with Bobby and I'm not going to do it again.

"Thanks, but no thanks," I say. "Let's finish our Cokes and go home. The waitress keeps looking at us like she wants to fill this table with people who are going to have more than Cokes."

Waitresses never seem to like kids. Not when there aren't parents around to leave big tips.

We finish up and catch the bus back.

I sit there quietly and try to imagine what it's going to be like when I come into the house with pierced ears.

My father will probably cut off my allowance and tell me how barbaric it is. I'll tell him I think football's really barbaric and we'll have a major fight.

Linda will want me to help her get hers done. Put a training bra on the kid and she thinks she's ready for anything.

Melissa will like them. If she's ever around to see them.

My mother will try to maintain the peace and tell me privately that it looks nice but that I shouldn't do things that upset my father.

By the time we get to Bonnie's house, her mother has returned from the tennis lesson. She keeps telling us how wonderful we look and then goes upstairs.

"She really is nice," I say.

Bonnie nods.

Ms. Alda comes back downstairs. "Here's a present for each of you." She holds out two sets of loops. They're just beautiful.

"Bonnie, your pair once belonged to your grandmother, your father's mother."

"They're gorgeous," Bonnie gushes.

Her mother nods. "I'll probably give you most of her jewelry. I really don't feel comfortable wearing it since the divorce. But I know that your father and she would be pleased for you to have them."

Bonnie's parents still get along even if they aren't together. Her mother and stepmother even get along. It certainly does seem strange to me.

"And the pair for you, Lauren, I bought with my first paycheck after the divorce. My first purchase on my own for the first time in years. I used to call them my independence earrings. I'd like you to have them."

Not just any pair of earrings. A special pair. For me.

I lean over to Ms. Alda, give her a kiss, and say, "Thank you."

She smiles and says, "Whenever you want to do something very brave, wear those earrings. I used to do that and it helped me through some rough spots. That's why I want you to have them."

I think about that. What a wonderful idea. What a very nice thing. She knows a lot about my family life. I bet that's why she did it. Now when I can put them in, I can think about independence and that there's someone out there who understands my need for it.

By the time I leave Bonnie's house, it's almost time for me to be home to set the table. I'm nervous, knowing that I'm going to be killed. Maybe my long hair will hide them forever. But if they don't find out right away, I'll have to stay scared until they do find out. I'll be the first person on my block with pierced ears and a nervous disorder. So maybe it's better to get it over with as soon as possible.

I walk into my house. Linda and my parents are sitting down in the kitchen.

"Guess what?" Linda yells. "Mom got a letter. She's going to be on a quiz show. She made it through the interviews. The one you like. The one where you can win up to twenty-five thousand dollars."

I sit down, making sure my hair is covering my ears. "That's wonderful. When?"

My mother says, "They'll be taping it in two weeks. Then it'll be on in about a month. Isn't that exciting?"

I nod. "That's wonderful."

"Wonderful," my father says sarcastically. "A chance to look ridiculous in front of millions of people. Folks are going to think I can't take care of my own family without sending my wife on one of those dumb shows."

My mother makes a face at him. "Well, Jack, maybe I'll do badly and only get a consolation prize. Would that make you happy?" She sighs. "I just don't understand why you think this is so awful. It'll be fun for me, something different. Even if I lose. But I'm going to try to win. If I did, we could do so much with the money. Send the girls to college. Go on a trip."

"You'll have to go yourself. I want nothing to do with whatever you win. We'll take a trip with my money, from my salary." He storms out of the room.

Linda says, "Why's he so angry? I think it's just great."

My mother shrugs. "He's just in a bad mood. He'll get over it. Why don't you two set the table? I'm going upstairs and rest for a while."

Linda and I get the dishes on the table.

"Did you hear the joke about the bed?" she asks. "No? Well, it hasn't been made yet."

It figures she'd think that one was funny. Hers hasn't been made in two months.

I decide to change the subject. "Hey, Linda. Guess what I did. But you've got to promise not to tell Mom and Dad."

She immediately comes over to where I'm standing. "Promise."

"I got my ears pierced." I lift up my hair and show her.

"Oh, wow, do you think I can get mine done too?"

Just then my father walks in and looks at us.

I drop the hair down, back over my ears.

Too late.

He starts yelling. "I thought I told you not to do that. Doesn't anyone ever listen to me anymore? How much did that cost you, young lady?"

I yell, "I paid for it out of my own money. I can do whatever I want with it. I have my rights."

"Don't you yell at me in my own house. I won't have it. When you start to pay rent here, you can do whatever you want. Until then, I'm still the boss."

The same argument. "That's it," I yell back. "I've had it. I know what I'm going to do. I'm going to sue you for malpractice, because you're such a lousy father."

My mother rushes in. "Can't I get any rest around here? What is it this time?"

My father and I both start yelling again at the same time.

He tells her how I never listen, how he told me not to get my ears pierced.

I scream that I never get to do anything I want to—not without a fight.

My mother says, "Both of you calm down. Really, there's absolutely nothing wrong with Lauren getting her ears pierced. Everyone's doing it."

My father shakes his head. "It's not right. You always side with the girls. I'm sick of it."

Sick of it. He should look at himself.

I run upstairs, leaving them to the fight that's beginning.

I lie down on the bed and think about it all. Can you sue your parents for malpractice? I'm sure going to find out when the new course starts on Monday.

Chapter 4

I check my earlobes out to make sure that they're not infected. I must have cleaned them out at least eighteen million times in the past two days.

I wish I could clean up the mess at my house. All the fighting is driving me nuts.

I haven't said a word to my father since the fight. I'm waiting to find out what my rights are in the new law course.

Morning announcement over the loudspeaker. "Will all teachers please check their phones. If they don't work, call the office immediately."

I look at Bonnie, and we crack up.

The bell rings.

Everyone rushes into the hall, past Ms. Lawrence, who is frantically trying to communicate with the front office on her defective phone.

Past Mr. Baxter and Ms. Daniels, who always look ready to hide out in the supply closet. Rumor is that he left his wife for her. And they always think kids don't know anything.

"Do you believe that idiot announcement?" Bonnie asks. She touches her bangs to make sure they're hanging down in her eyes.

"Typical," I say.

Finnegan, the Faculty Freak, is patrolling the halls, as usual. He takes hall duty very seriously. "OK, girls, move it," he bellows. He acts as if God personally directed him to get students to class on time.

As usual, we ignore him and go on in to biology class. My worst subject. It's a terrible way to start the day.

Erik Marks is standing at the door, pretending to look at his notebook. He's got this tremendous crush on Bonnie, but she prefers older men.

"Hi," Erik says and smiles. A rubber band from his braces shoots out of his mouth.

It's tough not to laugh, but he's a nice guy so I don't. Poor Erik. The same thing happened last year during his bar mitzvah. I hope his parents own stock in a rubber company.

We stand at the lab table.

Ms. Solomon passes out the frogs.

I want to puke.

I hate dissecting.

I hate frogs.

I hate the smell of formaldehyde.

I hate Ms. Solomon for screwing up my average.

Last marking period it was worms. Gross. Some of the boys used to put the spare parts in girls' pocketbooks.

"Now, class." Ms. Solomon raps on her desk with a pointer. "We've graduated to frogs. Isn't that exciting?"

No, I think. The only thing I'd like to dissect is Sandy Linwood. Her brain is probably smaller than the frog's.

"Put on your aprons now." She smiles.

I put on my puke-green lab apron. Robots. That's what we are. Robots.

Ms. Solomon comes over to our table, plops down a frog, and says, "I'm going to have to split the two of you up if you don't stop socializing this term."

It's kind of weird to wonder what a biology teacher who is obsessed with dissecting means when she talks about splitting you up.

I think to myself, "Big deal. Can I help it if guidance makes me take this because I'm college prep?" But I just stand there trying to look good.

She moves to the next table.

Someday she's going to be sorry. She'll have this awful lawsuit brought against her by the Frog Lovers of America and she'll need a good lawyer. She'll come to me begging forgiveness. I'll remind

her of the C that she gave me and turn her down.
She'll beg. Weep. Kiss my feet. But I won't change
my mind. They'll put her in jail for life.

Bonnie interrupts my thoughts. "Let's name him
Ferdinand."

I nod. It's as good a name as any. Ferdinand the
Frog. Last marking period the worm was Wini-
fred.

Ms. Solomon says, "Now quietly copy down the
diagram on the board."

I whisper to Bonnie, "Got an extra pen? Forgot
mine."

Ms. Solomon says, "Lauren, detention for talking. I warned you."

I say, "But I just asked for a pen to . . ."

She marks it down in the special book where
she keeps track of offenders.

I mumble, "It's not fair."

"Two days detention." She smiles and makes
another mark in her book.

I want to scream but I know she'll make it three.

Erik sneaks me a pen. He whispers, "Here,
keep it."

Ms. Solomon doesn't give him detention. She
thinks he's wonderful because he wants to be a
doctor and has this fantastic brain. The type that
always ruins the curve on a test. It's a good thing
that he's nice. I'm grateful for the pen.

I look at the pen. It has some writing on it:

Brush Your Teeth
Wear Your Elastics
Wear Your Headgear
HAPPY HOLIDAYS
from your
FRIENDLY ORTHODONTIST

No wonder he doesn't want it anymore.
Bonnie and I examine our frog.
Slime.
Disgust.
It's got beady eyes.
I hate it.
I only hope I don't get so sick that I have to go to the nurse and get sent home and miss the law elective.
I make it through the class.
I make it through the day until seventh period. Finally, the elective. I'm so lucky to be in the first group.
I rush off to the class. Bonnie rushes off to yoga. I take a seat right up front. Zack walks in and sits down next to me.
"Hi," he says. "Isn't it great, getting this course?"
I nod and try not to stare at his cheekbones. His eyes aren't bad either. Brown. Why must he be here?
The teacher walks in. Melissa's right. He's gor-

geous. Blond hair. Blue eyes. The longest eyelashes I've ever seen on anyone (except Señora Schwartz, our Spanish teacher—and she glues hers on every day). He looks like he could win an olympic gold medal in dimples.

He opens his mouth. "Welcome, class. I assume we're all here because we want to be. I've asked to teach this course. You've taken it as an elective. The reason that I am so pleased to teach this course is that I have been going to law school at night for several years. If any of you have similar plans to be lawyers, I hope this will help you decide what course to follow. Some of you may be here because you want to know what your rights are. I'll tell you from the beginning that great strides are being made in that direction, but there is still a long way to go. But you will learn things here that will help you to determine your own destiny."

Determine my own destiny. I love it.

He continues. "Laws are constantly changing. You are all going to have to become avid newspaper readers, if you aren't already. That will be an important part of this class. I also want you to know that I don't know everything, that we will all have to do research."

I decide then and there that I will do anything he asks. I think he's wonderful.

He says, "Let's go around the room. Give your name and tell why you took this course. It will help us get acquainted, and I'll learn more about the needs of the class."

A teacher who cares about our needs. I bet he wouldn't make me dissect a frog.

Ed Harmon starts. "I want to know my rights in case I ever get busted. I'm Ed Harmon. I want to know what the drug laws are and how to get around them."

Typical. Ed thinks he's the sharpest person around. I bet he doesn't even smoke grass or anything. He just thinks saying that will make him sound like a Big Shot. Even if he does, I don't think that makes him a big deal. He's so obnoxious hardly anyone can stand him.

A couple more kids speak.

Then it's Zack's turn. "My name is Zachary Davids. My friends call me Zack, but they're back in California. I'm here because I want to find out exactly what rights I have, whether I can go back on my own. I want to know if just because of a divorce, I've got to stay with my mother in New Jersey."

He says "New Jersey" as if it's the armpit of the nation.

I look at Zack while some of the other kids are speaking. Actually, I kind of look sideways so he doesn't know I'm checking him out.

He's chewing on his eraser as he listens to the other kids speak. Sandy brown hair. Brown eyes.

Those cheekbones. Blue jeans. A rugby shirt. He looks older than he is.

I think about Bobby and wonder what he's doing over at the high school. Probably making out under the bleachers.

All of a sudden it's my turn. I try to look intelligent to impress Mr. Matthews, and say, "I'm Lauren Allen. I want to be a lawyer and change the world." I decided not to mention malpractice suits right away.

He nods and then the rest of the class do their introductions.

At the end of the period, he says, "There will be a major class project. Either working alone or in groups of no more than three, I want you to specialize in one part of the law affecting children and young people. I also want this class to publish fact sheets informing the entire student body of their rights."

The bell rings.

Zack turns to me and says, "Maybe we can work together on the project."

I start to say no. I mean he's just an eighth grader. Then I think about how he seems so nice and all his friends are back in California, so I say, "I'll think about it."

I rush out to meet Bonnie at her locker.

Later on I see Zack. There are a lot of eighth-grade girls hanging around him.

I guess I shouldn't worry so much about whether he needs friends. He seems to be doing all right.

Detention with Ms. Solomon. I wonder how many years I'd get for slipping some arsenic into her Thermos of coffee.

By the time I get home it's time to set the table again. I feel like I spend half my life setting the table.

My mother's all excited. She's just bought the dress that she's going to wear for the television program.

"Oh, Lauren. Do you want to take the day off and watch it being filmed? If I win, you can all come running on stage to congratulate me. It'll be the most exciting thing that's happened to me in years." She's smiling. "And you know what? I've been thinking. Maybe I should start substituting in the school system. After all, I did teach before I was married, and I'm sick and tired of being home all the time. Even if I do win all the money, I've got to do something more with myself. I know your father wants me to stay home, but you're all growing up so fast. I realized it the other day when I saw Linda with the training bra. You don't need me so much anymore. You're all growing . . . and I'm not."

"But Mom! Subbing? The kids are animals to subs. And I'll just die if you come to my school."

"You won't die. Your father didn't die when you

got your ears pierced. You won't die if I come to your school."

I think about that. Maybe I am being selfish, and she looks so happy with her decision.

"Oh, OK," I say. "But you're going to be sorry. They tear most of the subs to shreds. Once one quit by third period. Just walked out of the building and never came back."

She smiles. "I'll do all right, and if I don't like it, I don't have to do it. But I want to try. Your father and I discussed it last night and that's what we decided. He doesn't like it much, but he realizes how important it is to me. And it'll be good to have more money coming into the house. It'll make your father less anxious."

"I don't want to talk about my father. I'm going to sue him for malpractice. I told him that the other day."

She smiles. "So I heard. Lauren, you've always been such a strange child." She's teasing me now. "Please try to remember we only want the best for you. I bet we can even prove that in court."

"Don't worry," I say. "I'm not really going to do it, sue you I mean. Well, at least not you."

She said, "Knowing your father, he'd probably countersue. Watch it."

"But I'm a model child."

"Trust me. We have evidence, too." She smiles. "Remember the time you filled his pipe with incense? And the time you cut one of his ties in half because you thought it was ugly?"

I remember. I was ten and he was wearing it and I walked up to him in front of company and cut it off at the middle. It was for society's sake that I did it. It was a crime for that tie to be seen in public.

She continues, "And the time you hid play money in the lamp and it caught on fire? And the time you made him feel just awful for running over the doll you left in the driveway?"

"But I didn't mean anything bad."

"The defense rests," she says. "He doesn't either. Try getting to know him. I'll talk to him again and see if I can get him to lighten up on you. Give him a chance."

Linda walks in.

"Melissa just called," she announces. "She said to tell you that she's staying at the dorm tonight with Cindy to study for an accounting test."

My mother frowns, but doesn't say anything.

Linda says, "If you win a lot of money, will you buy me some joke books?"

My mother hugs her. "Honey, if I win, I'll buy you a good comedy writer."

I hope she wins.

Chapter 5 _____

My mother doesn't win. She comes close but this guy from Hoboken, N.J., does. He's a free-lance writer so I guess he can really use the money, but it would have been nice if Mom had won. Then maybe we could have gotten the attic fixed up and I could have had my own room. And Linda could've gotten her comedy writer.

Now my mother's decided to sub for sure. Once she gets her papers in order, she's going to start.

At least I got the day off from school. No frog cutting for the day, and I did have fun thinking about what I'd do if she won. How I'd run up on stage, jump up and down, hugging her and yelling. How some Hollywood producer would be home with a cold, watching the tube, and discover me. But that didn't happen.

My mother did get some consolation prizes. The case of dog food would have been wonderful if

Gopher weren't so particular and hadn't refused to eat it. The vacuum cleaner would be OK if we didn't already have one that works, one of the few appliances that does. The year's supply of Pampers is useless to our family. How gross to think of my mother having another kid at this point. With my luck, she'd put it in Linda's and my room. The other consolation prizes were equally wonderful . . . two cartons of popcorn, and floor wax.

Now I'm back in school, and the day's started off badly.

I cut the frog's heart in half by mistake. When will this unit end?

Lunch was terrible, fish cakes and something masquerading as creamed corn. For dessert there were two pear halves in a paper cup.

By the time I get to law, I'm disgusted.

Zack says hello to me.

I smile at him but not too much. I don't want him to get the wrong idea. Sometimes I look at him and wish that he were in the ninth grade, but then I remember how I've sworn off men so I'm glad he's not.

Mr. Matthews is talking. "I want all of you to be on the lookout for proof that children are or are not granted rights. You should observe what's going on around you and read the newspapers daily. You've all got to be well informed if you are to be certain of your rights."

I think about how I have no right to refuse to work on the frog and wonder if the Supreme Court would rule in my favor. Allen vs. Frogface Solomon.

The class is given some free time to try to come up with some good ideas for the newsletter that we are going to put out.

I work with a group of ninth graders.

Every once in a while I sneak a look over at Zack. He's really excited about the project. His group looks like it's having more fun. The kids in my group, because we're all ninth graders, spend a lot of time trying to impress each other with how much we all know about things like drugs and sex and stuff like that. Half the time I don't think most of the people know what they are talking about.

When the bell rings, I rush out to meet Bonnie. She's going to get her hair trimmed and needs me along for moral support.

She's always sure she's going to ask them to trim off an inch, and they're going to make her look like a Marine.

We walk to the beauty parlor.

Bonnie says, "If it looks like they're going to cut off too much, promise me you'll scream."

I nod.

She always goes through this. Once when she was eight, someone cut off a little too much, and since then she's had this thing about getting her hair cut.

It's ridiculous. She's the kind of person who could have her hair messed up and half the kids in the school would rush out and have the same thing done to their hair. That's because, no matter what, Bonnie always looks fantastic.

She says, "If it's even a slight bit too much . . ."

"I promised. You know I will."

She grins. "I know. Look, Lauren, are you over Bobby yet? Dave says he thinks one of his friends would like you. We can fix you up and double."

Fix me up. It sounds like she's going to call in a cosmetic specialist.

"No thanks." I shake my head. "I keep telling you, no. Last time you did that, I ended up with Bobby. Never again."

She looks at me. "He wasn't so terrible. Come on."

Our only major argument. I don't see why my social life is so important to her.

I change the subject. "Mr. Matthews said to be on the lookout for any examples of kids not being allowed certain rights. Can you think of any?"

"You're changing the subject as usual," she says.

I nod.

"Oh, OK. I won't ask you to meet any of Dave's friends, at least not this week." She grins. "I've seen Zack looking at you. I think he's got a crush on you."

"Don't be ridiculous. He's just a nice kid," I say.

She's still grinning. "Sure."

"Look, why do you have to make something out of something that's not real?"

She shrugs.

We near the beauty parlor. She gets that terrified look on her face.

"It'll be OK. Just tell them you only want a trim. I'll watch."

She gets very quiet as we walk in.

They take her immediately. They know her and what a nervous wreck she is until it's over. I watch to make sure she doesn't end up with a crew cut.

I really wish my hair were absolutely straight. Once I even tried to iron it, but it got singed and I ended up smelling like a charred lamb. It's just no use.

I sit there and think about what she's just said. Maybe I should go out with one of Dave's friends. That way if Zack does have a crush on me, he'll know it's no use. I really don't want to hurt his feelings. He seems so nice.

Bonnie's hair looks perfect, as usual.

We leave.

"Want to go for a soda?"

I shake my head. "Got to get home. Mom said she was going over to the Board of Education to register to sub."

"She's really going to do it?" Bonnie groans. "Couldn't you talk her out of it?"

I shake my head. "It's going to be gross. I know I'm going to die if she ever subs for one of my teachers."

"Didn't you tell her what the kids did to Ms. Koster?"

Ms. Koster gave the kids an assignment and someone set fire to the garbage can. Then the next class turned all the desks upside down when she stepped out of the room. When she came back, they pretended nothing was unusual. By the time she got to her study hall, she was just about finished off. When they started to chant, she went nuts. She just sat there and cried for the rest of the day. Finally, they sent her home and had regular teachers cover the classes.

I nod. "I tried to tell her but she says she wants to try."

"Maybe if she'd won the quiz show, this wouldn't have happened. She'd stay home and not sub."

"Don't think so. She's going crazy at home. I think she'd do this anyway."

"I hope she survives." Bonnie tends toward the dramatic sometimes.

"Me too. Look, we've got to rush. I promised to set the table."

We do rush. But by the time we split up and I go into the house, my mother's already there.

The table's already set.

"Mom, I'm sorry I'm late."

She says, "So am I. What's going to happen when I go to work? You all are going to have to pitch in and help more."

I nod. There's not much I can say. When I know I'm wrong, I find it best to just keep quiet about it.

She says, "You can finish up. There will be only four of us. Melissa's staying at school again to study. Only pour the iced tea for the four of us. Your father should be home any minute, so get a move on."

"Where's Linda?"

"Upstairs practicing something for a variety show her class is putting on. She set the table before she went up."

Guilt. I always end up feeling such guilt when my mother is calm and doesn't yell when I do something wrong. She's got a way of doing that. Maybe it's something that comes to mothers easily . . . being able to make their kids feel awful without raising their voices.

I try to change the subject. "Isn't Melissa going to be around anymore? I never get to see her."

My mother looks at me. "Melissa's an adult now. She's got to lead her own life. Anyway, college is different. She's got a lot more work to do. And I don't want you to bring up that subject in front of your father. You know how upset he gets about it."

I agree.

My father comes home. He's in a pretty good mood. Insurance sales were good today. That makes him happy.

We get through the meal without a fight. The only time it's a little uncomfortable is when my mother talks about going to the Board office. But my father says something about how the whole thing's a passing fancy.

Linda tells four new jokes—bad ones.

After dinner I clear the table, do the dishes to atone for not setting the table.

Then I go to my room to think about Bobby. It's not that I miss him so much. It's just that sometimes it's nice to know that someone cares especially for you, someone who's not your family. I guess I wish there were someone like that for me, someone I was sure wouldn't hurt me.

The phone rings. It's Melissa.

"Lauren. Hi, how are you? Listen, tell Mom that there's someone on the phone. Don't let Dad know it's me. He'll only get on the phone and yell at me for not coming home for dinner."

I say, "Sure," and get my mother. I tell her to come upstairs. She does without asking why. I guess she heard the phone ringing and figures out what's going on.

I wish I were more sure of what's happening. When Melissa and I were real young, we fought a lot, but when we got older, we got closer. Now that she's been going out with Mike, she seems real distant. I think sometimes I'm jealous of him. She never used to act this way with any of her other boyfriends, but now that she's at college, she's different.

I try not to eavesdrop while my mother's out in the hall talking to Melissa. Sometimes I think my mother likes Melissa better than me.

She talks for a while and then goes back downstairs.

I was kind of hoping she'd come in and tell me what's going on. No such luck.

The phone rings again. This time I don't even get up.

Linda calls in, "Lauren. For you. A boy."

I go out. "Who?" What if it's Bobby, all kinds of sorry for what he did? If it is, I'm just going to hang up on him.

She shrugs and goes into our room. I bet she'll eavesdrop.

I pick up the phone. "Hello."

"Hi, Lauren. It's Zack."

Zack.

He says, "Hi, you still there?"

"Sure. What's happening?" I feel like an idiot, not sure of what to say. Why do I feel so dumb? He's only an eighth grader. Why do I feel so shy?

He says, "I've been thinking about the project Mr. Matthews assigned. I plan to do it on child abuse and want to know if you would too. I mean, when we discussed it in class, you said some good things and I figured we could do a good job on it together. It's a lot of work and I know you do well and take the class as seriously as I do."

I listen. He sounds older than he is. Older, more mature than most of the kids in my grade.

He says, "So what do you think?"

I don't know. "Let me think about it. I'll let you know tomorrow. That sounds like a good subject to me, but I'm not sure."

"Oh, OK." He sounds very disappointed.

"I promise. I'll let you know tomorrow."

We talk for another minute and then hang up.

I go back into my room and think about it. If we work together, I'm sure we'll both get A's. We're the best students in the class. We do both care about the subject. Also, our library's not that big and if we're both taking books out, there may not be enough to go around. Decisions. I also think about what Bonnie said about Zack having a crush on me. That makes me nervous. But he's a nice kid and I do like being around him. It doesn't have to be romantic. We can just be friends. Maybe I should work with him. Who knows? Why can't life be less confusing?

I lie down on the bed and try to think things out. Maybe I should call Bonnie and ask her to lend me Moose. Sometimes I think it's easier to talk to stuffed animals. They never hurt your feelings or confuse you.

Chapter 6

I've made my decision. I'm going to work on the project with Zack. It's silly to worry so much. It's just a project.

Next period's law. I'll tell him then.

I sit at my desk and think about Melissa. I wish she were around to talk to about all these things. I guess she and Mike are doing OK, that she's not afraid of getting hurt. I wonder why I turned out this way.

I can't even just have fun. I always have to worry and wait for disaster to strike.

The bell rings.

I go up to class. Zack's waiting outside the door. When he sees me, he grins.

I feel so glad to see him that I almost decide we shouldn't work on the project. That's how dumb I am, how scared.

"Well?" he asks.

I nod.

"Great." He smiles.

I smile back. Why can't I say anything?

We go inside.

Mr. Matthews is standing there talking to Ms. Richmond, the home ec. teacher. Bonnie found out they go together. I guess that's all right. She's really nice and he's too old for me.

After she leaves, Zack and I go up to him.

"Lauren and I are working together," Zack says. "We're going to do our project on child abuse."

Ed Harmon's standing nearby. "Yeah. And they're going to take some little kid, beat him up, and bring him into class to talk about how it feels."

"That's not funny. You're an idiot," Zack says.

"Why don't you go back to California and wait for the earthquake? Or wouldn't your father keep you? And who do you think you are, trying to make it with a freshman? You're just a punk kid."

The next thing I see is Zack taking a swing at him.

Ed punches him in the stomach.

Mr. Matthews moves in to separate them, but Ed keeps swinging. He hits Matthews in the face.

Zack punches Ed in the stomach.

Somebody runs to the phone and calls the office.

Ed takes another swing at Zack.

It's all happening so fast. I don't know what to do.

Ian Tomlin's holding on to Ed.

Zack's being held by Mr. Matthews.

"I don't want to see anything like this ever happen in my class again. We have to try to work things out without being physical. Now I want the two of you to calm down." Mr. Matthews' nose is bleeding a little.

The Vice-Principal, Mr. O'Brien, barges in yelling. That's the way he always handles situations. "What's going on in here? I demand an explanation."

Ed yells, "He started it. He hit me," and points to Zack.

"Wrong," Mr. Matthews says. "He didn't start it. You did, with your comments."

Ed says, "It's a free country. I have the right to free speech. He doesn't have the right to assault me."

Mr. O'Brien's yelling again. "You two are going to be suspended."

Guilty without hearing the story. It doesn't seem fair.

Mr. Matthews says, "I think that once you hear the extenuating circumstances, you may want to review the punishment for both. Zack was provoked."

Mr. O'Brien says, "You teach your classes. I'll handle the discipline."

"But . . ."

"All right, you boys, march right down to the office."

After they leave, everyone just stands there for a minute.

I hand Mr. Matthew a tissue and say, "Your nose is bleeding."

He says, "Thanks. Look, everyone, take your seats. I'll be back in a minute. Just sit there quietly."

He goes out and we all sit down.

I hate when something like this happens. Some of the kids like it, but I don't. School should be more exciting, but not like this. And I'm upset about Ed's comment about Zack's trying to make it with a freshman.

When Mr. Matthews comes back, I raise my hand.

"Yes, Lauren?"

"I don't think it's fair that Zack's going to get in trouble. Ed asked for it."

"Ed was just talking. It was Zack who started the slugging." That's from Ed's friend, John Miller.

"Ed's the one who hit you," Laurie Wilson tells Mr. Matthews.

"It's not fair," I call out. "Mr. O'Brien didn't listen to the facts. Isn't there any justice in this school?"

Mr. Matthews sits on his desk. "OK, now settle

down, everyone. Let's discuss this calmly, rationally."

That's one of the things I like about him. Most teachers would've told us to just take out our books and work quietly, pretending that nothing had happened.

Instead we get into a discussion about rules, why they are necessary and how to be fair about the punishment. Also about whether students have any rights in school or whether the administration can make all the decisions.

I can tell that Mr. Matthews didn't like the way O'Brien handled the situation, but that he's trying not to be unprofessional and tell us that. I sort of wish he would.

We spend the entire period talking about the rules of the school and the problems kids have had: accused of cheating when they didn't, unfair detentions, no say in the food served in the cafeteria, the classes that are required. After we talk about all that, Mr. Matthews has us examine what it would be like to be an administrator or teacher, how we would act. Then we try to make some decisions based on the entire situation.

It's a good class.

I'm sorry that Zack's missing it.

Maybe they'll take into account that it's his first offense and that Ed's a troublemaker. It's hard to know.

When the bell rings, I get up to leave.

"Lauren." It's Mr. Matthews.

"Yes?"

"When I talk to Zack after school, I'll tell him that you defended him. He's going through a difficult time. I think it's nice that you two are becoming friends."

I guess we are becoming friends, no matter what other people think.

There are a couple of kids standing around the desk, waiting for a chance to talk to him.

I say, "Thank you. See you around." Then I leave.

Bonnie meets me in the hall. "Is it true? Did you really have a fight in your class? Is Zack OK? What about Matthews? I hope they get Ed this time. Nothing like that ever happens in my class. The most excitement we've had was when Roberta Weinstein had trouble getting out of the lotus position and Ms. Sebold had to untangle her."

I nod. "I'd rather see that than what happened in my class. It was awful. I don't even want to talk about it now."

She changes the subject. "I saw David last night. He's got a friend he'd like you to meet."

I shake my head.

She pushes back her bangs. "Come on, Lauren. You can't spend the rest of your life staying home on Saturday nights."

"Thanks, but no thanks. If I want to do something, I'll let you know. Anyway, there are still parties and things to go to. I don't have to have a date to do things."

"Well, OK," she says, "but I know this guy would like you."

"Maybe someday," I say, to keep her from bugging me.

I wonder what's happening with Zack.

By the time I get home, it's late and I have to set the table, as usual. There ought to be a law against one kid getting stuck with all the chores. With Melissa out so much, I have even more stuff to do now and I'm tired of it. I think that I should directly receive the money that the government takes off my parents' income tax as a deduction for me. After all, when I was born, they got a free servant. That's my function in the family, to be the good one. I once decided it was the only way that I was going to get any attention. Now I think it's all taken for granted, and I'm expected to do it all.

Linda's lying down on the kitchen floor, with Gopher on top of her.

"What's going on?" I ask.

"I think he's got a tick on him and I'm trying to get it off. Want to help?" she asks.

"Yaag. I'll go set the table." I debate helping and

then bringing in the tick as an extra-credit project for Ms. Solomon but decide against it. It's not going to make any difference. Nothing's going to help in that class. She hates me, and when a teacher hates you, there's no hope.

Linda comes in just as all the dishes are on the table. "Hey, Lauren. Do you have a thumbtack?"

"What for?" I ask.

"Well, I have a toe, and now I have a tick." She holds up the wretched thing. "All I need is a tack to complete the game. Get it? Tick, tack, toe?" She falls down on the floor in a fit of hysterical laughter.

I wonder whether they will ever invent a medication that will cure her.

"Do you know what you get when you cross a dog with a hen?" she asks.

I step over her body and say, "Just this one, twerp. No. What do you get when you do that?"

"Pooched eggs." She's banging her fists on the floor and giggling.

"Don't you have any homework? Don't they make you do anything intelligent in fifth grade?"

She looks up at me. "Yeah, in health class today I learned where baby ears of corn come from."

"At last," I say, "schoolwork."

"Yeah, the stalk brings baby ears of corn."

"OUT!" I yell, just as my mother walks in carrying several boxes.

"What did you bring me?" Linda and I both yell at the same time.

She laughs and puts down her bundles. "Amazing as it may seem, nothing. I went to the shopping mall today and they were having a sale on clothes, and I finally decided to buy myself some things." She grins. "For me."

"What did you get?" I ask.

"A couple of pairs of slacks, a dress, and two sweaters. Lingerie. It's been so long since I bought something that I wasn't even sure what size I was. But I found out soon enough. It was great fun."

She starts taking stuff out of the cabinet. A quickie dinner. Spaghetti. Yeah. I love the way she makes it.

"I think that's great. You haven't bought anything since Melissa graduated from high school."

"And guess what else I did," she says. "I don't even believe I did it. I'm not even sure that I like it. But I think I do."

"What?" The suspense is killing me.

She pulls back her hair. Her ears are pierced.

I don't believe it. "Mom, when? Why? What's Dad going to say?"

She looks at me as if she doesn't believe it either. "I was walking past the store, looked in, thought about yours, and just went into the store. Before I realized it, I'd done it."

I giggle.

"I don't know what your father's going to say, but I don't think he'll divorce me for it. Anyway I decided I really need things for subbing."

My father walks in.

The packages are lying out there.

"What is all of this?" he asks.

"Things I bought to start subbing."

He doesn't look too happy.

"I'm going upstairs to start on my homework. Call me when dinner's ready," I say. I don't want to be around while they discuss this, especially when he discovers that her ears are pierced.

Linda says, "Me too."

Linda and I walk up the steps together.

I remember that I haven't checked my ears for a couple of days.

I feel them. Oh, no! Lumps!

We go up to our room.

I look in the mirror. The earlobes are infected. How gross.

Peroxide.

Q-tips.

I squeeze the earlobes.

Goop comes out.

It's almost as disgusting as dissecting a frog.

My body is diseased.

I can hear my parents fighting.

Maybe the infection's going to spread to the rest of my body.

I go into the bathroom and put on the stuff that Mom used when my toe was infected.

Maybe I've caught it in time. It might not have spread to my brain yet.

The phone rings. I run to get it.

Linda gets to it first. "And who shall I say is calling?"

She listens for a minute, bats her eyelashes at me, and hands over the phone. "For you. Someone named Zack." She stands there.

I say, "Would you please get the hell out of here? Oh, Zack, I don't mean you."

The kid doesn't move. I hate having the phone out in the hall, just because our parents wouldn't choose one room to keep it in.

"Excuse me for a minute," I say to Zack. "LINDA, GET OUT OF HERE!"

Zack says, "Did I pick a bad time to call?"

I laugh. "Around here there's no way of knowing what's going to be a good time. It changes from one second to the next."

"So what's new?" he asks.

Should I tell him that I've turned into a walking pus bomb? That my parents are downstairs arguing? I decide to ask about him instead.

"Not much. What about you? Are you suspended?"

"Yeah. I got one day and three generals."

Generals. That's the big-time detention where you have to put your hands on the desk in front of you and do nothing for forty minutes but stare ahead at the space in front of you. It's inhuman. Even teachers who you think are nice turn into animals when they have general. You've got to do something really bad or just annoy O'Brien to get it. I got it once and don't ever want it again. Mine was for throwing the piece of worm at Harry Warner, who put it in my purse. O'Brien wouldn't even give me the chance to complain. It was a victimless crime. You have to be human to be a victim, and Harry Warner isn't.

"What did Ed get?"

"A three-day suspension and five generals," he said. "Mr. Matthews came in and defended me, so O'Brien relented a little. Boy, do I hate this school. It's so full of cliques and unfair rules. I wish I had never come here."

I wonder why he's telling me this, and then I realize he probably just wants a friend. That's the other thing I do a lot, be everyone's friend, have them tell me all their problems. It's a little like the way that I do the work around the house. So that people notice me.

"Ed just got me so angry," Zack tells me. "That comment about beating up a little kid and bringing him into the class to talk about it. And then that comment about making it with you—that's none of his business. He's a . . ." There's a pause. "Anyway, I wish I'd really hurt him even though I don't like to fight. He deserved it. But now my mother's really upset because of the fight and she's grounded me. The only way I can get out of the house is for schoolwork, so I told her we were doing a project together and that I promised to go over to your house to work on it. I hope you don't mind, but I'll go nuts stuck in this house all the time."

I debate bringing him into my house and taking all the teasing that will go on. Oh, well, I can live through it. And I know how bad it is to get grounded. I do keep thinking about his saying it's none of Ed's business about making it with me.

"Sure," I say. "Why don't you come over after dinner? Or we can meet at the library."

"Let's do that," he says. "Meet you at the library at six thirty."

"Make it seven." I think of the dishes I'm going to have to do.

By the time I get downstairs, everyone else is already at the table and eating. My parents seem to have worked things out. At least things seem calm.

"Lauren, so who is this Zack?" Linda asks.

I sit down.

Everyone's staring at me.

"You're not planning to elope, are you?" That's from my father.

I get all set to yell until I see the smile on his face. Sometimes he's got a weird sense of humor. I'm not always sure what he's going to do, yell or make some dumb joke out of it.

"No," I say. "I thought I'd meet him behind the bushes, though."

"Lauren Allen, what way is that for a young lady to talk?" He's losing his sense of humor fast.

"Just kidding, Dad," I say. "Look, he's just a kid from school. We're working on a law project together."

"On suing your parents for malpractice?" my father says.

"No, on child abuse," I answer.

He chokes on a strand of spaghetti.

My mother laughs. "Surely that's not an accusation against us, is it?"

I shake my head. "No, it's just something I've become interested in and so is he."

My father says, "I've never met him, have I?"

Twenty questions time. My father thinks he's got to know everything about every guy who comes to visit or calls. Sometimes it gets embarrassing. Once he asked Bobby how many other girls he had dated and whether he had respect for me. I could have died right then and there. It was awful.

Melissa said that it was even worse when she started dating. Maybe that's why I'm so messed up.

"Look, Dad. He's just a kid, an eighth grader."

"One whole year," Linda says. "Big deal. I'm never going to get married."

"We weren't discussing marriage, just child abuse." I debate threatening her with the spaghetti spoon when I notice that she's eating hers with chopsticks. She's cornered the market on weirdness.

She says, "How can you stop a buffalo from charging?"

"Take away his credit cards," my mother answers.

My father turns to her. "You should know that one. Now that you're going back to work, I bet you're going to be spending like mad, living outside my salary."

"Why don't you just accept it and not feel so threatened?" My mother raises her voice. She hardly ever does that.

I can feel the knot in my stomach and I feel like I'm going to jump out of my skin.

"Who feels threatened?" he yells. "That's ridiculous. Just because you won't have to depend on me, need me anymore, why should I worry?"

So that's why he's acting this way. He thinks it's the money that makes him important. Sometimes I just don't understand his brain.

"Why can't you ever celebrate anything?" she yells again.

I throw my spoon on the table. That's it. I'm leaving.

Linda follows me out. It's like a revolution. Nothing like this has ever happened before.

I can hear him yell, "See what that job is going to do? It's making me unimportant to them, too."

I grab my coat and say to Linda, "I'm going to the library. Tell *your* parents I'll be back whenever I get done."

Linda nods.

I slam the door on the way out, hoping that the entire house will crumble and that I'll be left an orphan.

As I jog to the library, I wonder what kind of man acts that way. It's a good thing that I don't ever want to get involved. If that's what it's all about, I want no part of it.

Chapter 7

    I debate hitching a ride to the library. That would serve them right. I'll probably get kidnapped and hurt and then they'll be sorry that they caused me so much grief. The kidnappers would ask for a lot, though, and my father would say, "Oh, well, we'll just have to let her go. We have two others left, so what's the hassle? I never much liked her with the pierced ears anyway."

I keep on jogging and pass Donny Collins. He waves and calls out, "Hey, Lauren." I wave back and keep on jogging. Donny's the fleabrain who discovered that when you throw a hot paper towel up to the fire detector in the bathrooms, the fire alarm goes off. One day we had eight alarms and had to go out for each one of them. I caught a cold and my hair frizzed up. The school finally caught him, called his parents, and gave him generals for a month. They also had the fire department prefer charges against him. Then they had to explain to everyone how dangerous and expensive it was. Donny's reformed a little, but now he's known as "Smokey the Bear." He'll never live it down. Once you get a nickname like that around our school, it sticks for life. Or at least until you graduate and go away someplace where no one knows you and hope that no one from your past ever shows up and tells.

In front of the library is a whole bunch of kids I don't know. It's sort of a hangout, because kids tell their parents that they have to go there to work and then they just meet friends. If there's one thing I hate, it's walking past an entire group of unfamiliar kids who hang out with each other. I'm always afraid that they'll make fun of me, call me Frizzhead or something. That's the way some kids get, in a gang. They do things they wouldn't do alone.

As I pass them, I look straight ahead and recite the Gettysburg Address silently to myself. That way I look as if I don't even notice them. Having no eye contact is important in cases like this.

I make it. Inside the library. Safe in a place filled with books. And I'm even in luck. My favorite librarian, Ms. Jensen, is on duty. She's been helping me pick books since I was five.

I check the place out. No Zack. But I am really

early on account of having left the house before dinner was over. Maybe they'll make Linda do the dishes alone. Then they'll see how much I really do.

"Hi, Lauren Allen. How are you tonight? Read any good books lately?" Ms. Jensen always says that and she always smiles.

"No," I say, "I've decided to be a functional illiterate when I grow up."

"A noble ambition," she says. "But I doubt that. Not you. Not with your brains."

Ms. Jensen deserves an A in Librarianship. She not only knows her books, she knows how to make people feel good.

"And how's your family? I mean to ask Linda but she's always got her head buried in a joke book."

"My mother's going to work as a substitute," I tell her.

"How exciting." She stamps someone else's book choices, smiles at her, and says, "Enjoy them. See you soon."

"Mom bought some new clothes and had her ears pierced. I got mine done too, first."

She grins.

"My father's acting flippy about the whole thing," I say, not wanting to get too personal but wanting to talk to someone about it. "I just don't understand why."

She nods. "People get that way sometimes when things change. He'll survive, though. My husband did when I went back to work, when the kids all were in school. Now Mr. Jensen likes having the extra money and I have a job that I really love. So you see, it worked out well for us."

"I hope it works out OK for them," I say, playing with a lock of hair.

"I hope so too," she says. "Now, what are you here for? Anything special? May I help?"

"A friend and I are doing a law paper on child abuse. Where can I find the information?"

"Family relations, psychology, sociology, and law. Surely you know where those are?" She never lets me get away with not finding things on my own. Once she told me that she thinks it's more fun to check out the catalogue and wander among the stacks so that you have a chance to discover things. I still try to take the lazy way out, but she never lets me. She's always willing to help with recommendations though. I think it's turned into a game over the years.

I go to the card catalogue. Might as well do some of the preliminary research so that when Zack gets here, we can get started.

"Lauren," Ms. Jensen calls out. "We just got a new joke book in. Why don't you take it home to Linda?"

I look at her and cross my eyes. "I won't contribute to the delinquency of a minor. Do I have to?"

She laughs. "I think she's funny. Come on, admit it. You do too. With your sense of humor, you must."

My sense of humor. I guess she's right. I do have some good points on my own. With all the strong personalities in my family, I sometimes feel like a nothing. But I guess I do have some things going for me. I'm glad Ms. Jensen's there to remind me.

"Oh, OK. I hope they're better than her last set of jokes. She could drive me up a tree."

She says, "I'll leave it here and you can check it out with your books."

While I'm going through the card catalogue, I feel someone tug on my hair.

It's Zack. "I thought you were going to be later."

"Family problems," I say. "Had to make my escape."

He nods. "I know that one well. In California, I used to have to escape all the time. Now it's only sometimes."

I say, "There's not too much in here. Where else should we look?"

He says, "I got some books out of the school library already, and we can look in some of the real law books for sections on child abuse. Don't worry. We'll find stuff—and Matthews saw me after school at my locker and says he'll give us an extension since we can't work on it while I'm sitting in the generals.''

We go to the study section of the library and sit down at one of the tables.

I pore over some of the books. There are some interesting cases. It's sad though to realize that some kids are so damaged by their own parents. Physically. Not like the stuff that goes on in my house.

I look up and there are Bobby and Sandy, walking arm in arm. I want to die. Vanish. But I can't show it.

Instead I move closer to Zack and show him an article.

Bobby looks over and sees me. He doesn't look any more comfortable than I feel.

I'm not sure I'm going to survive this but I'll never let Bobby know how I feel. Actually I'm not even sure how I feel.

I keep talking to Zack, but have trouble not looking at them.

They sit down at the empty table near us. Sandy takes out a compact and puts on lipstick. When she looks up, she notices me, gives me a dirty look, then puts her hand on Bobby's shoulder.

I turn to Zack and say, "Do me a favor. Act like we go out."

He says, "Here?"

"Don't do anything extreme. Just act like it's

more than working on a term project. I'll explain later."

He leans closer to me and bites my earlobe, right near my pierced ear. I hope he doesn't get infected. Then he whispers, "Do you think I should get down on my knees and propose?"

I laugh.

He continues to whisper. "Is there anything else you would like me to do? I'm beginning to enjoy this."

"You're only in the eighth grade. You're not supposed to," I whisper in his ear.

He puts his arm around my shoulder and says, "I'm from California. We start earlier there."

That's it. I can't stop laughing. All of a sudden, I don't even care if Bobby's watching or not. Zack's crazy and I love it.

"We better get out of here before we disturb everyone else. Come on, we'll check out these books and come back tomorrow for more."

I nod. Out of the corner of my eye, I can see that Bobby's still staring at me and Sandy's poking him in the arm.

Zack and I get up. He grabs some of the books with one hand and holds my hand with the other.

We get to the checkout desk.

Ms. Jensen says, "Oh, it was Zack you were waiting for. How nice."

I blush.

So does he. But he doesn't stop holding my hand.

I wonder if there's any spaghetti sauce dried out on my hand.

When we get outside, past the crowd of kids, I say, "It's all right. You don't have to do this anymore."

He smiles. "Do I have a choice?"

I look at him. "Yeah, I guess you do. That means I do also."

He shrugs, "Women's liberation. That's fine with me. Especially if you don't let go."

I keep my hand in his.

I guess that answers his question.

"Look," I say, "I want you to know what that was all about. My old boyfriend was there with his new girlfriend and I . . ."

"Yeah, I know. Bobby and Sandy. A good lawyer always finds out all the facts beforehand." He grins.

I stop short.

"But you're in the eighth grade and I'm in the ninth."

He says, "That kind of junk doesn't matter anymore. Don't you want to go out with me?"

I think about it. Maybe I do. But what will everyone say? Even Bonnie will think it's weird.

It doesn't have to be anything serious. And I kind of like Zack. Who knows? For a person who planned never to go out again, this is awfully confusing.

"Let me think about it," I say.

"OK. Is hand holding off limits until the verdict comes in?" Zack says.

"I guess not," I say, not sure what I feel. "Listen, do you normally go home this way? Do you live near me?"

He says, "Not too far. About five blocks. I told you. A good lawyer always does preliminary research."

"Who have you been talking to?"

"And never reveals his, or her, sources," he says. "I plead the Fifth Amendment."

We walk along. It feels kind of comfortable being with him, sort of relaxed and friendly.

"There's something I want you to know about me," he says.

"Yes?"

"I don't want you to think I get into fights a lot." He looks nervous. "It was just that comment about child abuse and beating up a little kid."

We stop.

He lets go of my hand and stands there biting his lip. "Well, it's just that . . ."

I wait for him to continue.

"It's just that my parents got a divorce because my father used to do that to my brother and me all the time. That's why we moved so far away.

He's not allowed to see us anymore. That's what the judge ruled." He looks like he's going to cry. "My mother thought we'd be better off here where she grew up."

I don't know what to say.

He continues. "So when Ed made that crack, I just belted him without thinking about it. I hate to hit people. I just wanted you to know about my family. But please don't tell anyone else."

I promise and grab his hand. I don't know what else to say so I just hold on.

And I think I have it tough. There are so many people with problems you never know about. It's depressing. Especially to have it happen to someone you know and like.

We walk back to my house.

"Zack, there's something I've been wanting to ask you."

"What?" he says. "Ask me anything."

"Anything?" All of a sudden there's so much to choose from. I decide to stick to the original question. "Remember when you said you already knew about me?"

He nods.

"Well, how did you? Was it my charm, wit, and stunning appearance?" I pretend to model.

He grins. "No, actually it was books."

"Books?"

"Yeah, books. I moved here during a vacation

and didn't know people. So I spent most of my time reading books from the library. Almost every book I picked out had your name in it. Same with the school library. I figured we probably had the same interests. So I checked up on you a little. If I hadn't run into you and Bonnie that day, I would have met you some other way."

Books. I can't believe it. Books.

"You do have all the other things you mentioned," he says. "But I do wish you'd change one thing, though."

I wonder what it is. He must have discovered that I'm really a jerk or that I pick my toenails.

I wait for him to go on.

He says nothing, but smiles.

The suspense is killing me.

He's not going to say anything unless I ask.

"Well," I yell. "What is it?"

I stop, close my eyes, and wait to hear the worst.

"I wish you'd read a little faster. There are a couple of books I put on reserve that you have out."

I look at his grinning face.

The library. Ms. Jensen. That's how he found out so much about me. I bet she's got this secret hobby of matching people up by the type of books they read. Just wait 'til I see her.

We get to my house too soon. I wish we could have talked more.

"Look," I say. "Next time I'll invite you in but I don't think it's a good idea this time."

Zack says, "I'll talk to you tomorrow. Good luck with your parents."

He leans over and gives me a fast kiss.

He's going down the street almost before I realize what's happened.

I go into the kitchen, feeling confused.

Melissa's home. How unusual. She usually comes in way after my bedtime or says she's staying at the dorm. She and my parents are sitting at the table, having coffee and looking very serious.

I run up to her and hug her. I want to talk to her about so many things.

My father says, "Lauren, I want you to go up to your room immediately. We're in the middle of a discussion. I don't want to see you until I tell you you may come out. And then when you do, I plan to talk to you about your actions at the dinner table tonight."

I look at my mother. She's been crying.

Melissa hugs me and says, "I'll talk to you later, Lauren."

I leave. Once his majesty, my father, has spoken, that's it.

Linda's sitting on her bed, playing with her Barbie and Ken dolls.

I don't believe the positions she's put them in.

"Lin, what are you doing?"

She looks startled and separates them.

Maybe she does think about something besides lousy jokes. But I don't remember ever doing that with my dolls.

She says, "They make you come upstairs too?"

I nod. "What's it all about?"

"I'm not supposed to know, but when Melissa came in tonight, I heard her talking to Mom first."

"About what? What's going on? Is there a problem?" I ask.

"She's going to move in with Mike. Why did Daddy get so angry? On television they do that all the time."

Melissa's moving in with Mike. What am I going to do? Who am I going to talk to about Zack? What are they going to do with her room? Who am I going to switch clothes with? Is Melissa doing the right thing? Sometimes I feel like I'm part of a soap opera, only it's the real thing.

Now I know why Mom likes quiz shows and not soap operas. With quiz shows, you know right away whether you're a winner or loser. Once it's over, it's over. It doesn't work that way with things about real everyday life.

I think I like quiz shows better too.

I lie down on my bed. Will Melissa really leave home and live with Mike? Will Lauren go out with Zack and have to put up with the remarks from other kids? What will their father do? Will the Ken doll get the Barbie doll in trouble? Will my father forget to yell at me for running out of the house? Tune in for the next episode.

I bet the answers won't be easy.

Chapter 8

It's official. Melissa's moved out. She left a week ago. She and Mike came by today, Sunday, to pick up her stuff.

We weren't even allowed to stay in the house when they came over. My parents took Linda and me to some dumb movie. When we got back, I went into Melissa's room. It looks like a ghost town.

There's a note on the bureau for me. From Melissa.

Lauren:

I just want you to know that I love you very much and am sorry it's got to be this way. I don't want to get married until I'm sure it's going to be a good thing. I don't want to end up in a marriage like Mom's got. Please come visit Mike and me as soon as we get settled. Just call and

we'll make arrangements. Know that I'll always be around if you need me.
>   Love,
>   Melissa

I look at it for a few minutes and try to memorize the phone number she's written on the bottom.

There's also a note for Linda.

Linda comes into the room and I hand it to her and walk out. I figure she may want to be alone when she reads it. It's awful knowing that my father can get away with acting like this.

I don't even know what's going on in my mother's head. She looks like she's been crying but she hasn't said much, anything as a matter of fact. The whole time we were out she didn't say anything to anyone.

My father said enough for both of them though.

I hate him.

First I put Melissa's note in the shoe box under my bed and then I go downstairs to get a soda.

He's sitting at the table reading the paper as if nothing's happened. My mother's peeling carrots and slicing them as if she's chopping off their heads.

My father says, "Lauren, I don't want you to end up like your sister. In my day, a girl who moved in with someone would be called a tramp. I hope you realize that I have to do what I'm doing so that your sister doesn't set a bad example for you and Linda."

I want to kill him. I want to scream out that what about how Melissa's always making the honor roll, about all the volunteer work she's always done, about what a nice person she is. But I don't say a word. Neither does my mother, who's now tearing a head of lettuce to shreds.

It's a good thing he's never seen Linda play with her dolls.

He continues, "Perhaps if she and Mike decide to marry, things will be different."

My mother mumbles something to herself. I can't hear it.

I don't see what difference one dumb ceremony and a piece of paper are going to make. I think of all the people who do marry and end up divorced. Would he rather that happen to Melissa?

I go upstairs. I know if I stay there we'll get into a gigantic fight.

I'm afraid to even bring Zack into the house. With the names my father's called Mike, I don't think he's ever going to want to see another male visitor in this house.

My parents should have had only boys. Better yet, they should never have gotten married; then I wouldn't have had to go through this.

My father said he's going to make Melissa's room into a study. The only good thing that could have come out of this is that I could have had my own room—the only good thing. And then he says that. My mother said we should leave the room the way it is, that Melissa should be able to come back if things don't work out.

Now my parents aren't speaking to each other.

This house is a terrible place to be. I go to sleep.

When I wake up, it's morning. Time to go to school. It'll be better than being home.

I think it will. But I'm not sure what's going to happen once people figure out that Zack and I are hanging around together. Maybe they'll think we're just friends. But I don't even know if that's all we are.

I haven't even gotten up enough nerve to talk to Bonnie about it, and she's my best friend.

I check out my earlobes. They're better but not good enough to put in the earrings that Ms. Alda gave me, the independence ones. I hope they get better fast. I'm going to need all the help I can get. In another week I should be able to put them in.

I sneak out of the house without even having breakfast and go over to Bonnie's.

We walk to school. On the way, Bonnie says, "Lauren, Dave said that Bobby saw you at the library with some guy last week. He asked Dave who he was. Dave didn't know, so he asked me. How come I don't know?"

This is it. Faster than I thought. I was so sure

I'd have more time to think about it. "It's Zack. We're doing a law project together."

Bonnie frowns. "Dave told me that Bobby said you acted like you were going out with him."

I don't say anything. We're almost at school.

Bonnie says, "Lauren, you just can't go out with Zack. Everyone's going to think you're some kind of creep who can't do any better than an eighth grader. Come on, I can fix you up with someone else."

I turn to her. "Look, I don't need to be fixed up with anyone else. Sometimes you act like I could never get a boyfriend without your help. And I think Zack is nicer than anyone else I know. I don't even know if I am going out with him. I just know that I like being with him. Is that such a crime?"

"At this school it is," she says. "Nobody but a creep would go out with someone younger."

I turn to her. I've had it. Her attitude. My father's attitude. It's all getting to me.

"So now I'm a creep. If that's what you think, we don't have to be friends anymore. I know how you'd feel, hanging around with someone who's a creep."

I storm off and go to my locker.

I want to cry.

My best friend. If she feels this way, what's it going to be like with everyone else?

Word spreads fast in our school.

Go to the library once with someone, walk down the halls, and people have you practically engaged.

Mindy Donner comes over. "Hi, Lauren. I hear you're robbing the cradle these days."

I turn around and look at her.

She's smirking.

I walk past her without saying a word and go into homeroom.

Bonnie's already in there, talking to someone else as if I don't exist.

If that's the way it's going to be, that's OK with me, I think.

But it's not really OK. She is, was, my best friend. What am I going to do? In a few days, my sister moves out and I lose my best friend. And to top it all off, people say I'm robbing the cradle. That makes me nervous. Mindy's got a whole group of friends who follow whatever she does. When she's nasty to someone, they all are. And here I am, with Melissa gone and my best friend not talking to me. All because of Zack and I'm not even sure of how I feel about him. What if he and I don't end up friends? I'm not going to have anyone, not anyone who's real important to me.

The bell rings. Biology. Wonderful. Bonnie's my lab partner, and we aren't even talking to each other.

We get to the class, put on our lab aprons and

go to our table. Silence. Then Bonnie whispers, "You don't have to be so touchy."

"You called me a creep."

Ms. Solomon says, "That does it. The two of you have detention for whispering. Now, I'm splitting the two of you up. Bonnie, you will work with Mitchell. Lauren, you with Erik."

Erik comes over to my table.

Bonnie goes over to Mitchell's.

Great. Now Erik is going to find out that he's got a frog mutilator for a partner and that I'll probably mess up his work. Then he'll hate me too. I hate Biology. All these weeks on one dumb frog —and all those charts she makes us do in class— when will it ever end?

I want to take the dissecting instrument and plunge it into my heart.

Instead, I just stand there and watch Erik Marks, F.M.D., Future Medical Doctor, start working on Ferdinand.

He looks at me and says, "What did the two of you do to the frog? It looks like you could be arrested for frogslaughter."

"It was dead when we got it. I plead the Fifth."

He grins at me.

Ms. Solomon comes over. "What seems to be the problem?"

Erik says, "No problem. But do you think we could have another frog?"

She nods. "I knew you would disapprove of this work. I put you at this table to make sure that Lauren learns something."

She goes to get another frog.

Erik whispers, "I hope you don't mind. I don't want to get you in trouble. It's just that this frog would be impossible to work with and I really do want to do this right. If I'm going to be a brain surgeon, I've got to start somewhere."

I nod. "It's OK. With the way my life's been going, this is minor."

Ms. Solomon brings the frog and then goes to check on someone else. It's amazing. She doesn't say a word when Erik and I talk, just when Bonnie and I did.

"Do you mean all that talk about you going out with Zack?" Erik asks.

"How do you know already?" I can't believe it.

"It was the homeroom topic for the day. Look, most of the kids in this school act like morons. Zack's in the chess club. He's nice," Erik says.

I vow never to make fun of rubber bands popping out of Erik's mouth. We work on the frog. This time I can actually see the different parts of the frog before they're all sliced up.

When the bell rings, I walk out before Bonnie has a chance to call me a creep again.

Someone comes up to me in the hall and puts a

hand on my shoulder. I jump. It's Zack. He's grinning.

I do like him. I really am glad to see him. I look around to see who's watching. Some people are. They are also whispering.

Zack notices too, because he says, "Lauren, how about tucking me into my cradle?"

I look at him. He's grinning and acting as if he doesn't care who hears. He's even acting as if he enjoys the whole thing. No wonder. I bet no one's calling him a creep. It makes me laugh though. There are still some people who are trying to listen.

I sigh. "OK, Zack. I'll do it, but I'm getting sick and tired of having to pick up your teddy bear every time you throw it out."

He says, "I promise I'll only throw out the rattle."

We walk away from everyone else and go stand in a corner of the hall, near the guidance office.

I say, "I guess you've been hearing stuff too."

He nods, "Mostly from the eighth-grade girls I didn't pay any attention to. The boys think I'm really something, though." He's grinning.

"Doesn't it bother you?"

"No. Last year, in California, a lot of my friends were older. And anyway, I like you. I don't care about what anyone says."

I think about that. I wish I could be that way.

And then I remember how Zack reacted to what Ed said. Maybe it's not as easy as he makes it sound.

Finnegan comes up. "All right, you two. Get to class."

We both rush off.

It's a difficult day. In Spanish class Julia Simpson tells me I must really be hard up for a social life. I turn around and tell her that if she calls going out with Andy Bradford social life, she's in serious trouble.

Bonnie and I don't even sit together at lunch. She's already sitting with someone else, so I go off and sit at a table by myself. I feel like the whole world is staring at me and there's no place to hide. By the time I get to law class, I'm exhausted, just wiped out. Zack sits down and says, "How's it going?"

I shake my head.

Mr. Matthews starts the class. There's no time to talk. We spend the entire period making assignments for the fact sheet. I volunteer to write an editorial about the rights of students who get detention without a fair hearing.

When the bell rings, Zack and I walk out together.

He says, "Want me to walk you home?"

I nod yes, and then I remember. Solomon's detention.

"I've got detention. Biology."

LIBRARY
NORTHEASTERN JUNIOR HIGH

"I'll hang around and wait for you. After last week's generals, I'm used to staying late."

He walks me to my locker, then down to biology. I can't believe how many looks we get. Sometimes I wish I went to a really big school where everyone didn't know everyone else's business.

Bonnie and I have to sit there and listen to Ms. Solomon give us a lecture about how we're letting our friendship get in the way of our academic lives. She should only know that we aren't even speaking to each other. Then we have to write a hundred times each, "I will not use biology class time frivolously."

I get done before Bonnie, turn in my paper, and leave. Zack's waiting outside.

He says, "Why don't we go over to my house and work on the project? My mother's got a date right after work, so there'll be nobody there to bother us."

I think about what my mother will say about that and decide it doesn't matter. I don't even care what my father thinks, not the way he's treating Melissa.

I nod.

We walk over to his house. It looks smaller than most of the others on the block. I guess that's because there are only two people living there.

Once inside, he's a little nervous all of a sudden. "Listen, can I get you anything? A Coke? An

English muffin with peanut butter and jelly on it? That's what I always have when I come home."

"I think I'll just have a Coke. Do you have a special place you want me to hang up my coat . . . or should I keep it on?"

He laughs. "Think you'll feel safe taking your coat off?"

I laugh too. "If that's all I have to take off."

We sit down in the living room after he brings in the Coke and hangs up our coats.

The living room's decorated beautifully. I wonder what his mother looks like, is like, how she'd feel if she knew I was here. So I ask, "How would your mother feel about your entertaining an older woman in the house all alone?"

"She's not going to care," he says. "Look, I don't understand what the big deal is. Some of those kids are so dumb. What's it matter to them what we do? And anyway, one of the guys my mother's dating is two years younger than she is, and no one makes a big deal about it."

"She's not in the ninth grade, with him in the seventh. It's different, maybe, when you get older."

"Look," Zack says. "I haven't had to wear Dr. Dentons in years. This whole thing is silly. Do you know how to play backgammon?"

I nod. "I thought we were going to work on our project. Do you always lure women to an empty house to play backgammon?"

He grins. "Only the ones who look like they can play it well."

"I play to win."

"That's OK," he says. "So do I. Play to win. It'll be fun."

I jump up. "Where's your phone? I've got to call my mother and tell her I'm going to be late."

"Why don't you stay for dinner? Then we'll have time to work on our project too."

"I'll ask her."

I call. She says that it's OK. I neglect to mention that Zack's mother is out on a date.

We play backgammon for a while. He wins the first game. I win the second. And the third. He doesn't seem upset that I've won, just glad that we both play well. Bobby used to get angry when I did anything better than he did.

Zack makes the dinner: two chicken pot pies and chocolate ice cream for dessert.

During dinner, I tell him all sorts of things I didn't think I could talk about. Like how much I miss Melissa, how mean my father can be, how I hate sharing my room. He's real easy to talk to.

He tells me how much he misses his older brother, how hard it was to move, and how he still loves his father, even though he can't see him. He says it's hard when you love someone and hate him at the same time.

I can understand that.

We clean up the kitchen. There's not much to do when all you've had is chicken pot pies and chocolate ice cream.

Neither of us mentions the way some people act because we're together. I feel sort of funny bringing it up again.

"Lauren, all my books and my desk to work on, all that stuff's up in my room. Do you want to go upstairs and work on the project?"

"In your room?" I ask.

He nods. "Unless you want to help me carry the books and the desk downstairs."

I laugh. "How heavy is the desk?"

He pretends to look very serious. "Very heavy. It took the moving men, all four of them, two hours to carry it up. And one of them ended up with a hernia and we had to perform an emergency herniactomy on him, right here in this house, right on top of the desk."

"I'd hate to see that happen to you," I say. "Biology's not my strongest subject. We'd better study upstairs," I say. "By the way, is herniactomy a word?"

On the way up, he says, "I just made it up. Sounds good, though, doesn't it?"

We go into his room. It's really nice. Rock posters all over the walls. A skateboard and surfboard in one corner. A large, but not that large, desk. A bureau and matching bed. A bed. What if

Zack's like Bobby? Why am I up here? What if my father finds out that I've been alone with some guy in his bedroom. He'll throw me out, turn my half of the room into an extension for his study.

I must be staring at the bed a lot.

Zack says, "Lauren, come on, I promise it's OK." He pulls two chairs up to his desk and sits down on one of them. He opens one of the library books. "Now, stop worrying. What's the problem?"

I sit down and open one of the books.

We work quietly for about five minutes.

Then I say, "Listen, I used to go out with a sex maniac."

Zack smiles. "Me too."

"Somehow I think we have different reactions to the same situation," I say.

He says, "Look, do you want me to sign a contract stating exactly what I will and won't do?"

"Let me learn more about law and contracts first. Then we'll do that. I don't want to be taken advantage of by an unscrupulous future lawyer."

He pretends to be smoking a cigar, doing an imitation of Groucho Marx. "How would you like to be taken advantage of by a scrupulous future lawyer?"

All of a sudden, I'm not so nervous. Zack's not Bobby, and I'm not even the same Lauren who went out with Bobby. I'm different. This is something new. Not all guys have to be alike. I mean even when I really thought Bobby was wonderful and that it was real true love, I never felt this "nice" about the whole thing . . . I never thought that Bobby and I were friends, just that we went together. With Zack, I feel like I've got a friend.

"Better watch it," I say. "If we're ever going to be able to open law offices, we better do well in this course."

He shakes his head. "Somehow I doubt our careers are going to depend on a junior high project. But OK, I'm ready to get to work."

We start working on the project.

Each of us takes half the books, skims them, and decides which ones are going to be the most useful.

Zack's really working hard.

I'm the one who's sitting there, trying not to think about what it would be like to make out with him. I also begin to wonder what the problem is—doesn't he think I'm as attractive as the last sex maniac he knew?

It's all too confusing.

Maybe I should just solve this once and for all by taking him in my arms, throwing him on the bed, and doing all sorts of things that my father would never approve of.

Zack looks up at me. "What are you thinking about?"

I can feel myself blush.

He says, "Me too."

He leans over and kisses me.

I kiss him back.

It's very nice.

It's also very uncomfortable trying to make out, sitting at desk chairs.

We move over to the bed and sit down.

"Are you sure this is a good idea?" I ask.

"Positive," he says, and grins.

"OK, but we can only make out for five minutes," I say.

He laughs. "Should we set the timer my mother uses for baking . . . ? Or how about a stopwatch?"

I laugh. "The timer. That way we don't have to stop to check it out."

He tries to look very serious. "I thought maybe you'd want to be absolutely accurate, not go a second over five minutes."

I nod. "I'm willing to give up a slight bit of accuracy for the sake of the sound of the timer."

He rushes downstairs for the timer, rushes back, and sets it.

While he catches his breath, I check that he's got it timed right.

He does. "On your mark, get set, go," he yells, throwing himself down on the bed.

I just stand there.

"Come on, Lauren, you're wasting valuable time."

I sit down on the edge of the bed.

He sits up.

"You must think I'm crazy," I say.

"A little. But you play backgammon well and read good books."

"Is that why you like me?"

He nods. "Couldn't you have asked me this before we set the clock radio?"

"Yeah, but then I couldn't have wasted the time. Are you getting mad at me?"

"Maybe later, after the timer goes off. Not now. I don't want to waste the time."

I look at him. He does have great cheekbones. But that's not enough reason to make out with someone. At least not for someone who's been as sheltered as I have been. No wonder Melissa left home.

I like him. I want to be held by him. I feel so lonely without Bonnie and Melissa to talk to. And I like being with Zack. He's nice and attractive and bright and funny.

I lean over and kiss him.

He's definitely much nicer than Bobby, makes me feel different. And he likes me even if I am messed up about making out.

When the alarm rings, we both sit up.

"What about the time we missed while you were talking?" he asks. "Can't we count that like a time out in basketball?"

I shake my head. "Look, I've got to get home

before it's too late. I don't want to get my parents angry at me."

He nods. "OK, let's go. I'll walk you home."

We get our coats.

I look in the mirror. My frizzy hair is definitely not neat. I take a comb out and put lipstick on.

"Did you have to do that before I kiss you good night?" Zack says. "That looks like one of those flavored lipsticks I hate."

It is flavored, strawberry.

"For one so young, you certainly do know a lot." He grins.

I take out a tissue and wipe the lipstick off.

He gives me a kiss.

"Is this the good night one? I thought you were going to walk me home," I say.

"This is the good night from my house kiss. After I walk you home, I'll give you a good night from your house kiss. Maybe along the way, I'll give you a halfway there kiss." He starts counting on his fingers. "Then I can have one for the road . . ."

"Enough!" I grin at him. "If you don't walk me home soon, all you'll end up with is a fight with my father."

"Is your father very strong?" Zack asks as we walk out of his house.

"Very strong. And very mean. I'm thinking of suing him for malpractice."

Zack starts to laugh. "That's wonderful. Of course, I don't think you'd win. But could you imagine what it would be like if everyone were able to sue their parents for malpractice?"

I nod. "But my mother says my father would countersue if I took him to court."

He grins. "I'd be a character witness for you."

"You mean you'd come to my defense."

"Yes." He leans over and kisses me.

We stand in the middle of the street for a minute.

"I'm almost home. We better get there so that my parents don't get mad and say I can't see you anymore."

"You really are afraid of them, aren't you? They've got you trained."

He makes it sound like I'm a dog or something. But I think about it. They do have me trained, better than Gopher. I come in when I'm supposed to, try hard to be a good little girl. I practically do everything but roll over and play dead. I'd probably even eat the case of dog food my mother won, if they asked me.

We get to the door. This time we go inside, even though I'm nervous.

I introduce Zack to my parents and Linda.

Linda says, "What's red and dangerous?"

"A herd of stampeding apples," Zack answers.

Linda grins and sticks her tongue out and touches her nose with it. That's her very special trick, a sure sign that she's impressed with Zack.

Zack grins at her.

I can see her falling in love with him the way I used to fall in love with some of the guys Melissa used to bring home.

My father asks us, "Well, did you get work done? Let me see it."

My heart drops. "We left it at Zack's."

"I can run back and get it to show you," Zack says. "If you wish."

My father shakes his head.

My mother asks him some questions about where he used to live, how he likes it here, basic parent questions. It seems to go all right.

I walk Zack out to the porch. "If my father had said he wanted to see all the work, what would you have done?"

Zack whispers, "Thrown myself under a passing truck."

I grin. "Well, we're OK so far. He hasn't killed you or me."

We give each other the good night from my house kiss, and I go back inside.

My father says, "Just remember what I told you. I don't want to see you end up like Melissa."

I want to scream that I don't think Melissa's done anything wrong, but I don't want to get into another fight with him. Sometimes I think the only way to handle him is by pretending he doesn't exist. That seems to be what my mother is doing. She hardly talks to him anymore. Maybe that's not the best way to act, but it's the only one that seems to work with him.

I say, "Well, I guess I better go upstairs and wash my hair. Good night."

I go up to my room.

Linda's sitting there, not doing anything.

"What's wrong?" I ask.

"Nobody's ever around anymore. Melissa's moved and now you don't come home until late."

"But this is the first time," I say.

"Yeah, the first. But not the last, I bet." There are tears forming in her eyes. "I'm going to be the only one left in this house, 'cause I'm the youngest. And things are getting worse."

I hug her. There's not much else I can do. She's right. Things are getting worse. And she will probably be the last one out.

I want to tell her things will end up fine. I want her to tell me that also. I end up hugging her and saying nothing.

Chapter 9

Announcement over the loud-speaker. "Will all teachers please check to see if their phones are on the hook. Someone's is off and the buzzing is driving everyone in the office crazy."

That's it. The school's office staff has finally flipped. It was bound to happen, having to deal with the whole student body, administration, faculty, and parents. I knew all it would take some day would be some kid sneaking the phone off the hook and letting it buzz. Since the front office can't tell where it's coming from, they have to track it down over the loudspeaker.

I look up. Ms. Lawrence is holding the cut wire from her phone. The receiver is missing. Someone from our homeroom has done it.

She sends one of the kids to the front office to report it. Then Mr. O'Brien arrives, screaming that unless someone confesses, we'll all have detention forever.

It's not fair.

I raise my hand and tell him so, and that we have some rights.

He says, "You're students. While you're in this school, you must do what you are told."

Bonnie speaks up. "It's not right to punish the entire class for the work of one criminally minded fiend."

"Criminally minded fiend" makes me laugh.

Bonnie laughs too.

I really miss her.

O'Brien extends our homeroom time.

He searches all the boys, and the nurse searches all the girls. Finally, it's found. Ed Harmon's got it hidden inside his gym sneaker.

The bell rings and everyone but Ed is allowed to leave. No one apologizes to the rest of the class for the accusations and search.

I walk out the door. The fire alarm rings.

How gross. It's damp outside. My hair's going to get all frizzy. I'm probably going to catch pneumonia. It's cold, and we're not allowed to go to our lockers for our coats.

I walk outside. Behind me someone says, "Stay away from our eighth-grade boys. Stick to someone in your own class."

I ignore the comment, but from behind, I hear someone call, "Lauren."

I turn around and there's Mindy Donner smiling. "I just want you to know that I think it's fine that you're going out with an eighth grader. I mean, if that's the best you can do . . ."

Before I have a chance to say anything, I hear Bonnie say, "You are the lowest of low. I think you're just jealous that Lauren's going out with someone nice and bright and cute. The only reason you get to go out so much is the free movie passes your father is always giving you."

Mindy turns and walks away. I can tell that Bonnie's comment got to her.

Bonnie confronts me. "Now can we talk? You've been avoiding me."

"Avoiding you? It's you, not me," I tell her. "You haven't talked to me at all."

"Wrong." She shakes her head. "You're the one who walked away just because I was sitting with someone else. You could have joined us. It's never bothered you before. You haven't said anything or sat with me at lunch or called at night. What am I supposed to do? Not say what I think? But that didn't mean we had to stop being friends."

I think about it. She's right. I did do a lot of the pulling away. "But you think I'm a creep now, right?"

She shakes her head. "No, I don't. But I do think you are making things hard on yourself by going out with Zack. Look what's happening. People are being awful. You must like him very much."

I nod.

She puts her hand on my arm. "Well, that's good enough for me. And I think he's nice. If you'd given me the chance I would've told you that before. Come on. I don't want to fight."

"Me neither. I'm sorry."

She smiles. "Apology accepted."

We get to biology a few minutes late. Detention. Back to the old days. It's even worth the detention. I'm glad Bonnie had enough sense to make up. I don't know why I didn't. I feel overwhelmed, I guess.

After class, Bonnie says, "Let's throw a party, the two of us. We'll invite kids from all different classes. That way everyone will get a chance to know each other. The only thing is that when I tell Dave, he's going to want to invite Bobby and Sandy."

Bobby and Sandy.

I'd almost forgotten they existed.

"That's OK. It doesn't matter," I say. "At least, I don't think it does."

She says, "It's a deal then. We'll have it at my house. My mother won't mind buying the stuff for it. We'll get together tonight and make up the guest list."

"I think that's a great idea," I say. "And listen, thanks."

She grins. "I'm doing it because you didn't snitch

on the time I almost fainted after getting our ears pierced. And anyway, Moose misses you."

Things are better for the rest of the day. It's good being friends with Bonnie again. And she helped me realize that I haven't been giving people the chance to let me know that they don't all feel the same way about me going out with Zack.

Law class. The kids from my homeroom who are in the class discuss what happened in homeroom, how we all got accused and searched. We decide to include the incident in the newsletter that's supposed to come out next week.

After class, I tell Zack about the party Bonnie and I are planning.

He frowns. "I hate parties. I don't want to go."

"Why not? It'll be fun. You'll meet a lot of new people."

"I don't want to meet a lot of new people, at least not at a party. I hate parties. Come on, Lauren, we can just go to a movie or something."

I don't say anything, not all the way home.

He keeps trying to get me to smile. I don't want to. In fact, it takes everything I have not to cry. Life's not fair. Just when I think everything's straightened out.

"Look, Zack, I'll talk to you later," I say as soon as we're at my house. I go into my house without really saying anything else to him.

I wish I had someone to talk to who wasn't directly involved. I go up to my room and lie down on the bed. Melissa. If Melissa were here, I could talk to her. I go under my bed and pull out the shoe box to find Melissa's phone number. I lie back down on my bed and try to think everything out for myself.

No matter what I do, nothing seems good. Bonnie and I make up and she wants us to throw a party and Zack doesn't want to come. Either way, one of them is going to be mad at me. And no matter what happens at school, I never have any rights. And all of those kids are being mean to me.

I start to cry. I've just got to call Melissa. She's known me all my life. And she said she'd be there if I wanted to talk.

I go out into the hall, making sure no one is there—although I have this feeling that my mother wouldn't mind.

As I dial her number, I try to calm down. I hope she answers, not Mike.

She does. "Hello?"

I start crying immediately.

"Who is this? What's going on?"

I try to catch my breath, so she doesn't think it's some kind of "phoney," a kid calling to fool around. "It's me, Lauren."

"What's happened. Is anything wrong at home?"

"Nothing's wrong. It's just me." I try to get calm. "I feel bad about everything. I want to talk to you."

"Is it any one thing?" she asks.

"My life's a shambles," I wail. "I miss you. I need to talk to you."

"Do you want me to come over and get you?"

That's more than I hoped for. "Oh, yes, please. How soon can you get here? But how can we do it? You know what Dad said about you never darkening his doorstep again."

Melissa says, "Look, I'll meet you outside. That way I don't have to come near his doorstep. Anyway, I've been to the house during the day to see Mom. He just doesn't know that."

I didn't know that. And Mom's never said a word.

Melissa continues. "Mike's studying for an exam. I can use his car. I'll be there as soon as possible."

"OK." I feel relieved somehow.

"I'll meet you down the block. That way you won't have to put up with a scene. Just get Mom aside and tell her where you're going, so she won't worry."

We hang up. I go downstairs. My mother says, "Honey, what's wrong? Have you been crying?"

I say, "I'm OK," but I go over to the sink where she's washing dishes. No one else is in the kitchen, but I don't want to take any chances. My father might have the place bugged.

I whisper, "I'm going over to Melissa's for a while. Don't worry."

"How are you getting there? Are you sure everything's all right? Don't you want to tell me? Maybe I can help you."

"It's OK," I whisper. "I just want to talk to her. She's picking me up on the corner soon."

My mother nods. "Tell her I'm still trying to get your father to relent, to realize he's not being fair."

I can't say anything to her about that. If I were her, I wouldn't let him get away with murder, the way she does. I wouldn't let him treat his daughters so badly.

On the way out the door, I run into Linda. She's carrying library books.

Oh no, a new set of jokes.

"Did you hear the joke about the roof?" she asks.

I decide to go along with it. Melissa can't be at the corner yet. "No, I haven't heard the joke about the roof."

"That's just as well. It's probably over your head."

I leave before she has a chance to say any more. I stand on the corner, hoping Melissa gets there before my father gets home. I just hope he has to stay late writing up some insurance policy. Maybe they'll invent a new policy to be given at birth to kids. If things turn out badly, they can collect on insurance and have a chance to start over.

Melissa arrives.

I get into the car, hug her, and start to cry again.

She says, "Put on your seat belt. We'll go back to the apartment and talk."

"But Mike's studying for an exam. I don't want to bother him."

"It's OK. He said we should come back there. He studies in the living room. We can talk in the bedroom. It's my place too."

"Oh, OK."

She turns a corner. "Want to stop for some ice cream on the way home?"

I'm confused until I realize she means on the way to her home, not mine. I nod again. If I open my mouth, I just know I'll start crying again.

"Applegate's has a brand new flavor." She smiles at me. "Watermelon fudge ripple with cashews."

My stomach lurches. "You're kidding, aren't you?"

She nods. "Yes. I'm kidding."

I smile at her. "You almost got me that time."

"It wouldn't hurt." She's still smiling.

We ride along in silence for a few minutes.

Applegate's. I get a cone, one scoop of banana, one of cherry vanilla coconut. Melissa gets a single dip of raspberry with sprinkles. We drive on. The ice cream starts to drip a little. I'm probably the slobbiest ice-cream eater in the world.

We pull up into a parking lot right next to a railroad station. "That's my apartment building over there." She points to it. We cross the street and enter this sort of courtyard, with some trees, which is not very well kept.

"Hi, Melissa." A couple of really cute guys are walking down the steps.

She nods and says, "Hi. This is my sister Lauren."

I want to die. I look awful from crying and now I'm probably covered with ice-cream drippings. They both smile and say hello. Melissa and I continue to walk up the path.

She says, "They live right above us. They're on the hockey team. Sometimes they practice at home. Once Mike went up and threatened to ram a hockey puck if they didn't stop. Another one is a weight lifter. Sometimes he drops the weights. There are times I could kill them, but they're usually pretty nice. Wild parties though."

I wonder how she can take it. We go in one of the doors. "We're one flight up," she says.

I can hear people yelling in one of the downstairs apartments. We get up to her apartment. She takes out a key and opens the door. Mike looks up from his books, smiles, and says, "Hi."

Melissa walks over and kisses him on the forehead. I look away.

"Lauren and I are going into the bedroom to talk. First I'm going to give her the grand tour."

Grand tour. We can walk through the entire place in a minute and a half.

"This is the living room." There's not much of it. A single bed with large pillows on it, a desk, and the stereo.

"The kitchen." Lots of plants, a folding table and a couple of chairs, and a midget refrigerator. The stove and sink. Also two cats.

"Lauren, meet Batman and Robin." Cats. I didn't even know she liked cats.

"The bathroom." Small. But it's got everything you need.

"The bedroom." Two bureaus. One giant bed. Giant! A rocking chair. And that's it. Except for the bamboo shades.

"Sit down on the bed. I'll hang our coats up." She goes over to the closet. I plop down on the bed and roll over on my side.

She giggles. "I forgot to tell you. It's a water bed."

I kind of roll back and forth on it. Then I giggle. "Can you actually sleep on this?"

She nods. "At first I thought I was going to have to take motion sickness pills to survive, but now I like it a lot." She comes over and sits next to me. The bed sort of rolls around and then settles down.

"Now what's the matter, Lauren? Let me try to help. Is it Dad?" She's biting her lip.

"Oh, it's OK. I feel better now."

She says, "Oh no, you don't. You're not going to

avoid it. If you were so upset, you really should talk it out."

I decide to level with her. After all, she's my only choice. I tell her how hard it's been with her gone. How things are developing between Zack and me. About not talking to Bonnie. How we made up and how she wants to have a party. And how Zack says he doesn't want to go. The tears have started. I can't stop crying.

Melissa holds me.

"I wish I were dead," I cry. "Nothing ever works out for me. Or I wish I could run away like you did and get my own apartment."

She holds me until I calm down. "First of all"— she shakes her head—"I didn't run away. I walked. I'm nineteen, and Mike and I had been talking about the move for a while. We were together for a while. And you're right, I did want to leave home. I've wanted to for a long time, but I didn't until I thought it was right. Do you really think it would be right for you now? And do you think you're doing what's best about Zack?"

"You mean I shouldn't go out with him. Is that what you think?"

She shakes her head. "No, I don't think that at all. I remember when Tracey Mitchell went out with someone who was younger. They had a rough time. But they both thought it was worth it. So they just kept going out. It took a couple of years, but eventually everyone accepted it. If you want to go out with Zack, I think you should. In fact, if you want we'll have both of you over to dinner."

I sigh. "He probably won't come here either."

"Did he say that he positively wouldn't go to the party or that he didn't want to go?"

I think. "Didn't want to go."

"Did you talk to him about it or just get mad and act the way you did with Bonnie?" Melissa asks.

She knows me well. "I didn't talk to him, just got mad."

She shrugs. "Maybe you should try to find out why he doesn't want to go. It's probably been difficult for him too."

I think about it. She's probably right. A party with lots of new people and when all those people may not approve of you—well, it's just not easy. But it's not going to be easy for me either.

She says, "I think you should talk it out with him. I know it's hard, but you've got to. Lauren, it's difficult for people like us, coming from a family where nothing is ever discussed, where nobody can talk about what's really going on. And nothing's ever direct. I always thought all the fights were because of money. But that's not it. Mom and Dad use that as a weapon against each other instead of talking about the real problems. I didn't realize that 'til I moved out. Now, with Mike, I have to be real careful not to do some of the same things our parents do in fights. It sounds like you've picked up some of their bad habits."

"Like what?"

"Not finding out what's really bothering a person, not really trusting others, not showing real feelings. It's hard to change our behavior. But we've got to. It doesn't work for our parents. It won't work for us."

I think about it. It's so hard to understand myself, let alone what's happening in other people's heads.

Melissa says, "You don't have to be perfect. You couldn't be if you tried."

I smile. "Not even if I try real hard?"

She shakes her head. "And no one expects it. Zack cares about you. So does Bonnie. I do. And you're just going to have to accept the fact that some people need to make themselves feel bigger by putting others down. They think you're an easy target because you're going out with someone younger. Don't let them get to you."

"Doesn't it bother you that Daddy's so awful to you?" I ask her.

She nods. "I used to cry about it a lot. But I'm doing what's right for me now. I've had to learn that there's no easy way. But I've also learned that a person can survive if she does what's right for herself in spite of what others think."

"Are you happy?"

"With Mike?" Melissa smiles. "Very. But we work hard at the relationship. It doesn't come easy."

"Did you ever go out with anyone younger?"

She giggles. "Yeah, Mike. He was born two weeks after I was."

I laugh. "Maybe it runs in our family."

"Somewhere, right now, there's an eight-year-old just right for Linda."

"Do you think so?"

She shrugs. "Maybe Linda's going to end up with someone who's ten years older and people will complain about that. Who knows? But I bet it won't be easy for her either, no matter what. It's just a myth, a fairy tale, that relationships are easy. Look, would you like to stay for dinner? Call Mom and tell her." She strokes my hair.

"My hair's frizzy," I say.

"And mine's too straight. I've always been jealous of yours. Want to trade?" She tickles me.

"No. I guess I'll keep it."

I call home. My mother answers.

"Mom, I want to stay here for dinner. Think we can manage it?"

She says, "Sure, Lauren, if you want to eat at Cindy's and then study, that's fine with me. Just be sure to be home by nine thirty."

For a second I think she's gone off the deep end.

I don't even know a Cindy. Then I realize. He must be standing nearby, and since I don't know someone by that name it's a safe alibi. If she said "Bonnie," we'd be in trouble if Bonnie called.

It's really lousy that we've got to lie about all of this. Just because he's so strict.

"Well, thanks, Mom, see you later." I hang up.

Mike, Melissa, and I sit around and talk.

They're really nice to each other. They listen to each other. It sounds like they do try to work things out. Maybe I can learn to do that. Bonnie and I managed to get our problems straightened out. I bet Zack and I can try. I hope it works.

Why do people have to act so dumb and always pick on other people? Maybe kids outgrow it, but I don't think so. I know a lot of adults who act the same way. But Mike and Melissa try not to. And Bonnie. And Zack. And me. And some others. Maybe there's hope. Not for everyone. There's no hope for my father. There's no hope for Mindy. There's no hope for those rotten eighth-grade girls who make fun of me. When I become a lawyer, I'm going to try to get an amendment to the Constitution passed, outlawing meanness.

Chapter 10

When I get home, Linda tells me that Bonnie called, and Zack's called twice. "Boy, he certainly sounded like he wanted to talk to you. I hope someday someone wants to talk to me that much."

I call him back.

"Lauren, I hate large parties. They drive me nuts," he says immediately. "Couldn't you ask me to do something easier, like spend the night in a cage with boa constrictors?"

"How about doubling with Bonnie and Dave? Would that be easier?" I think of that as we talk.

"Anything," he says. "But do you think they'll want to be with me? I mean, isn't Dave in the eleventh grade? A junior isn't going to want to double with an eighth grader."

"I don't know," I say. "I'll find out. I just wanted to check with you to see if it would be OK, since I did the other thing without discussing it with you, and it caused a real mess. I'm sorry."

He says, "I'm sorry too. If it's really important to you, I'll go. But I hate parties where I don't know anyone, and with everything else that's going on, I just don't think I can stand it."

"What else is going on?"

He says, "Do you have any idea how many kids are betting on us? That we're going to break up. That we're going to stay together. Charlie Kaletsky has started a pool, like football, only we're the game."

"Are you kidding? What did you say when you found out?" I gasp.

There's silence on the other end for a few minutes.

Oh, no. I bet he slugged Charlie and is going to get into trouble.

"Well," I yell into the phone. "Well, what happened?"

"Promise not to get mad?" he says.

Oh, I knew it. He's gotten into another fight.

"Please tell me. I want to know."

"We have to go together for twenty-two years. That's the number I took in the pool." He laughs. "Twenty-two years. I'll split the winnings with you."

I have to laugh, too. "Zack, how could you? Bet in a pool about us."

"I figured I had the best inside information. And we could just fix it. What's twenty-two years?"

Incredible. We've practically just met and he's betting on twenty-two years!

We talk for a few more minutes and then we hang up so that I can call up Bonnie. She answers immediately. "Guess what. I just about have the guest list made up. It's going to be so much fun."

I'm afraid she's going to kill me, but I've got to tell her. "Bonnie, I spoke to Zack about it, and he just can't stand big parties. Would you be really angry if we doubled instead?"

There's silence on the other end. Oh, no. Our friendship is over again. I can't stand it. Finally she speaks. "I'm not sure about the doubling. It's OK with me. I'll have to check with Dave. And I can throw the party myself. But even if Zack won't come, will you?"

It's the least I can do, and anyway, it's been a long time since I went to a party.

She says, "Listen, do you have any idea how long the two of you will be going out?"

What a strange question. And then I remember. The pool. Not my best friend too.

I say, "Zack bet twenty-two years. He promised to split the winnings with me. What kind of deal can you offer?"

She giggles. "Sixty-forty? And I'll go with you when you get your ears double pierced."

Double pierced. My ears still haven't stopped

dripping from the first time. Fat chance I'll be doing that.

"Look. I'll think about it," I tell her. "But seriously, you're not upset about the party?"

"No," she says. "When I talked to my mother about it, she said we hadn't planned well. I told her the whole story about what's been happening, how you and Zack have been getting picked on by some of the kids. Then she asked me if we'd consulted Zack. When I said we hadn't, she told me this might happen. I guess she and his mother have been talking about it."

It's nice to know that some people understand.

"Then it's OK?" I ask.

"Sure. I'm just glad we're still friends."

"Thanks," I say.

My mother comes upstairs. "Lauren," she says. "It's late. Bedtime."

I hang up after saying good night to Bonnie.

My mother says, "Your father figured out that I was covering for you. I'm not a very good liar. He also figured out that I've been using some of the food money to give to Melissa. I guess he's known for a while, kind of, but just now decided to let me know—especially when he realized that we're both going against his wishes. He's in a terrible mood. Also angry because I start subbing next week. Just stay clear of him, though. He promised me he won't yell at you for going over there."

"Why does he have to be so awful?" I ask.

She shrugs. "He really thinks he's doing this for everyone's best, that he's got to make everyone's decisions for them. For years I've been able to get him to do things by letting him think they were his ideas, but this time he's been impossible."

I say, "How can you stand it?"

She shrugs and walks away without answering.

Twenty-two years. Zack bet twenty-two years. That's longer than my parents have been married. I can't see how some people manage.

I wonder what I'll be doing in twenty-two years, whether I'll end up like my mother or any of the other mothers I know.

Twenty-two years. I won't be living at home again. I won't be going to school again. I'll really be on my own.

I wonder if I'm ever going to marry. Have kids. Really be a lawyer like I want to. It's hard enough to know what it's going to be like tomorrow, let alone that far in the future. It's even a little scary thinking about it. Like what I'll be doing. Where I'll be living. Whether I'll live long. Will my parents be around when I get older? Or what if they die? Who will care about me then? Even though my father's sort of a lousy parent, I know he does care about me. What if he has a heart attack and dies? I'd be upset. And who'd take care of my mother? I'm not sure she can take care of herself. What if I do have kids and they hate me and won't listen? I wish there were a mail-order catalogue you could use to get the kind of life you want, so that there would be no questions, no wondering, no worrying. And if you weren't happy with your purchase, you could get a trade-in on the old life-style and buy a new one.

At night, that's what I dream about. Some guy, like a car salesman or an insurance agent, trying to pressure me into buying a life-style I really don't want.

I'm really glad when the alarm goes off and it's time for school. I dress up a little. Now that Zack's at school, I take a little more time, put on a little mascara and lipstick. I mean, what if he decides that he's made a mistake or something? By the time I get over to Bonnie's house, I'm running a few minutes late.

She rushes out. We walk quickly. She says, "Did you hear the news? Bobby and Sandy broke up."

I smile. I can't help it.

"Don't you have anything to say about that?" she asks, rearranging the bangs on her forehead.

I just keep smiling.

"Come on, Lauren. Say something."

I smile. "Couldn't happen to two more deserving

people. What happened? Did he develop an allergy to her pom-poms and megaphone?"

She says, "He decided they just didn't have enough in common."

Ha! I could have told him so.

"What if he wants to ask you out again? Would you go?" she asks, trying to sound very nonchalant.

I think about it. Going out with Bobby again. Being able to go out on dates in a car. Seeing R-rated movies more easily. It would mean not going out with Zack. Not having to deal with everyone's abuse.

"Well?" She asks.

I have to know. "Did Bobby ask Dave to have you find out the answer?"

She stops short. "Come on. What makes you think that?"

"Is it true? He did ask, didn't he?" I'm smiling.

She says, "My lips are sealed. Dave would kill me if I said that it was true. So I'm not saying anything."

That's good enough for me. I grin. She doesn't have to say it out loud. I know it's true.

We walk silently to school.

I think about it the whole time. Going out with Bobby again. Why should I even want to when Zack is so nice? Why should I still care about Bobby? Why do I want to go out with him?

School. Homeroom. Bio. The frog's almost finished. Solomon tells us there's going to be a test next week.

I hate tests that I have to really study for and will probably do lousy on no matter how much time I spend. I wish my brain were all-around useful, instead of just in some things.

On to law class. Zack's waiting at the door for me. It's the first time I've seen him all day.

"Where have you been?" I ask. "I kept looking for you in the halls."

"Would you believe a secret spy mission for the Intergalactic Council?"

I shake my head. "Try again."

"Searching the world for the perfect wave."

"And you found it already? Where's your surfboard?"

He grins. "In my locker. No, really I had a doctor's appointment. My yearly checkup."

"Anything wrong?" I'm always terrified that something's going to happen to someone I care about.

"Nope," he says. "Perfectly healthy. Guaranteed to last at least twenty-two years. Just think of how much interest we'll have in the pool in that time. We'll be able to go to Europe on our winnings."

Twenty-two years again. What if I do decide to go back with Bobby? How's Zack going to feel? How will I feel? Why did Bonnie ever tell me?

I decide not to think about it. "Europe? On the

interest? Don't you think we should put the money away for a rainy day?" I listen to myself. It sounds like something my father would say. Yeech!

Zack shakes his head. "Oh, no. By that time, we'll have made it through lots of rain. At the most, we'll use a little of it to buy an umbrella to take with us to Europe."

Mr. Matthews comes out. He puts his hand on Zack's shoulder. "Want to help fold the law newsletters? They just got here. Both of you worked so hard on this, I think you'll be pleased."

We rush in. The newsletters look great. We did work hard to get them done. The kids who typed them did a fantastic job, hardly any errors. We all read the articles for a few minutes. We've already read them in class, but it looks different all done on mimeograph and everything. Professional. Like the real thing.

Then we fold them. Two sheets. Information on both sides. Editorials. Articles. Cartoons. All about laws that affect young people. Some things about what happens at the school.

As we're folding, Mr. Matthews tells us we've done a great job, most of us. We all know he's thinking of the creeps like Ed who didn't do much, trying to con their way into getting a passing grade. But I don't think it's going to work in this class. "I will evaluate each of you on your understanding of the material, the way you wrote it up, and your participation in class. I'm extremely proud of most of you."

We applaud ourselves.

"We'll get these all folded, counted out, and placed in homeroom mailboxes. The homeroom teachers will pass them out in the morning," he says. "I just want you to remember we're publishing some things that are going to cause comments and maybe even anger."

"Will you get fired?" someone asks.

I think of the articles—about the administration, and the teachers who give unfair detentions, stuff like that. Even though the articles are unsigned, I bet some of the people are going to try to find out who's responsible for which writing. And then they'll blame the student and Mr. Matthews. He'll get into a lot of trouble, I bet.

He shrugs. "I've got tenure. They won't be able to fire me easily. I can use the law to help me. Don't worry. I've made the choice, and I hope there won't be a problem. If there is, we'll just use the experience to learn how to best deal with the situation."

I look at Matthews. He's brave. I also know that he's almost done with his law studies, and will soon take the bar exam to become a lawyer. It must be easier to do something like this when you know you're not going to be around much longer anyway. It's a shame the way a lot of the good ones leave and go on to other things. The good ones who stay almost always have outside jobs. I don't know who made the rules that teachers get paid what they do. It's not fair that Solomon and Matthews get the same money and everything. Maybe that's why Matthews went into law—to try to make things fair in education for everyone.

I also look at Zack. He's so nice, so much fun, so cute. I must be crazy to even consider going out with Bobby again.

I am crazy. I'm still thinking about it. I don't know what to do. Maybe I should call Melissa tonight.

But she hasn't even met Zack yet. And anyway, I know what she's going to say, that I have to do what's best for me. How can people always know what's best for themselves? Damn.

We fold all the papers. The bell rings. Some of us sit around and plan strategies in case there is trouble. Something tells me the administration isn't going to be too happy about the newsletter. Finally, everyone gets up to leave.

Zack says, "Let's go over to my house."

I grin. "To visit your timer?"

He laughs. "With any luck. Could we set it for seven minutes?"

"Six and a half."

"It's a deal," he says.

We go over to his house. His mother's home already. She's gorgeous. Long curly brown hair.

Curly, not frizzy. Cheekbones like Zack's. Green eyes. No wonder he looks so good. And she acts as if she doesn't even know how beautiful she is. If I had a body like that, I'd be so grateful.

She says, "Hi. Welcome home."

Zack says, "I thought you were working late tonight. And then going out."

She shakes her head. "A change in plans."

"Oh."

She gives him a look. "Does this ruin your plans? I should hope not. Aren't you and Lauren here to study?"

I could just die of embarrassment. But not Zack. "Mostly," he says.

She smiles. "Mostly? Well, why don't you two have a soda with me, then you can study, and Lauren, you're invited to dinner. Zack's told me about you. So has Bonnie's mother. I've really wanted to meet you."

We all sit down and talk. Ms. Davids is very nice. And funny. A sense of humor a lot like Zack's. I guess he takes after her.

It's fun except I keep thinking about the six and a half minutes. It's awful to think about how much you want to make out with someone when you should just be thinking about things to say to his mother for the first time.

I can tell Zack's mind is not totally on the conversation either. He keeps looking at his watch.

"I can tell that the two of you are anxious to study. I can remember what it was like to be young and want to study." She's grinning. "You two may go upstairs, but don't study too hard. I'm serious about that."

Zack laughs. "Got you. OK, Mom, we'll see you later."

Zack and I go upstairs and sit down on his bed.

"Somehow I don't think she expects us to study the whole time."

He grins. "We're just not supposed to study too hard. That's her way of telling us not to do too much."

"I can't believe she's a mother."

"I can. I live with her. Since she's got to be the only parent, we talk a lot. She knows I like you a lot, but she also told me we're too young to do too much. I told her I know that."

"Can you really talk to her about all of that stuff?" I think of my mother.

He nods. "Yeah. But I still don't tell her everything. It's not good to tell parents everything. You've got to do some things on your own and learn to be your own person."

"That sounds really good," I say. "For one so young, you really know how to handle yourself."

He says, "Don't tease. You'll be sorry."

"What are you going to do?"

He leans over and tickles me. I tickle him back.

He kisses me. I kiss him back. The timer! I've forgotten all about it.

"Zack. Stop. We've got to set the timer."

He says, "Don't worry. I've got an automatic one that goes off in my head."

"So do I. That's why we've got to set the timer. Somehow I don't trust the one in our head."

He grins. "Five minutes the other day. Six and a half today. By next week, we'll be up to an hour."

"Fat chance. Look, we have to be good."

He just grins.

"I didn't mean that kind of good."

He just keeps on grinning. I just sit there for a few minutes until he gets up and sets the timer. I wonder if his mother has noticed that it's vanished.

I look at him and think of Bobby. It's so confusing. Why should I think of Bobby when it's Zack I really like.

He comes back and sits down again. "What's wrong?"

"Nothing," I say. "Come on. The clock's ticking away."

He looks at me. "What's bothering you? I never know what's going on. Sometimes you act happy with me. Sometimes you don't." He looks at me. "Come on. You can tell me." Then he grins. "Is it my mouthwash? My deodorant? Do you hate rugby shirts?"

I smile. "No. I've just got other things on my mind."

"Like Bobby and Sandy breaking up?"

"How do you know about that?" I can't believe it.

He says, "One of the girls at school made sure it was the first thing I heard when I got back from my doctor's appointment. Before I even got into the office for my pass, she came running up to me in the hall to tell me."

I don't say anything.

"That's it, huh?" he asks.

I just sit there, confused.

"Do you want to go out with him again?"

I start to cry. "I don't know. I don't think so. But then I keep thinking about all the trouble we have because we go out, and I don't know what I want, what's best for both of us. I just don't know."

He says, "I think it's worth it. You're the best friend I have."

I think about that. Zack's one of the best people in the world. Nicer than anyone else I've ever gone out with. More fun. More considerate. But I hate the way everyone is making a fuss about us going together.

I'm the kind of person who just likes to fade into the woodwork, not stand out in a crowd or anything. And going out with Zack makes me stand out. People are taking bets on what I'm doing.

Girls are making nasty comments to me in the hall. I'm just so confused.

He says, "Look, do you want to be alone for a while to think things out? I'll go downstairs and help my mother get dinner ready. You can think about everything."

I nod. He gives me a kiss and leaves.

I lie down on the bed and cry. He's so good. Why did he have to be born a year too late? Why did I have to be born a year too early?

I just lie there and try to sort things out. The alarm goes off. I'd forgotten about it. Six and a half minutes and we didn't use any of it. I don't have an answer yet.

Why couldn't my parents have raised me to be sure of myself and to know what to do? I really do wish there were a way to sue them for malpractice. Then I could hire advisors who could tell me what to do, what would be the best for me. But I can't.

And I'm not sure that even advisors can answer this one for me. I wish Bobby and Sandy had never broken up. I wish I weren't so confused. I wish that most of the world would vanish and let me live life the way I choose. I wish I really knew how I want to live.

I hope that when I come back reincarnated, I come back as a piece of pickled herring. Somehow I don't think pickled herring has as much to deal with.

Chapter 11_____

All hell's broken out in the school. The newsletter came out.

The Principal and the Vice-Principal practically had heart attacks when they saw it. Ms. Solomon vowed to track down the writer of the editorial on unfair detentions. Some of the parents are pretty upset. Some aren't. My father wants me to drop out of the class, but I won't.

Some of the teachers are furious. Some aren't. Mr. Matthews is pleased. He says that we did a good job, and now everyone is more aware of the issue of children's rights.

Some people want him fired.

I'll be glad to graduate and get out of this school. I hope the high school's better. Except that Zack's got another year here. It's like I get paroled a year before he does.

I still don't know what to do. Bobby called last night. I'm going to see him tonight. I've told Zack.

He said OK, but I know he's upset. I would be too. I am upset, in fact.

Bobby sounded so nice over the phone, telling me how much he'd missed me, what a mistake it was to break up with me for Sandy. He told me how great it would be if we got back together. How things would be different. How the good things would be even better now.

I told him I wasn't sure. I told him that I was willing to talk to him, but that there would be no guarantees.

He said he was sure that once we saw each other again, everything would be fine.

I just don't know. I've got no idea what's going to happen. So far tonight I've tried on eight different outfits. None of them looks right for the occasion.

I finally decide on blue jeans and my gray sweat shirt. That looks very casual, not like I'm trying to impress him or be sexy or anything. Sort of like I'm making time to see him between jogging engagements. I also wear the independence earrings Bonnie's mother gave me.

Linda's sitting on her bed staring at me. "Don't you have anything better to do?" I ask her. "You're making me nervous."

She shakes her head. "Do you think there'll ever be a time when I have to make the choice of two guys? Sometimes I don't think there'll ever be one."

"Don't worry," I say. "It'll happen. Sixth-grade boys just mature later than the girls. Boys always do, well almost. There are exceptions." I think of Zack and wonder what he's doing tonight.

She says, "Do you think I'll ever be as nice-looking as you and Melissa?"

It's so funny. I don't think I'm that nice-looking.

I say, "You look wonderful now. Don't worry."

She lies down in her bed and stares at the ceiling. "John Pollack asked Judy out. He's in the sixth grade."

Judy again.

"Linda, do you really care about going out because you want to or because other people in the class are starting to go out?"

She sighs.

"Well?"

"I don't know. A little of both, I think."

"Don't you think you should just relax a little and then do what you really want to do?"

She looks at me. "What about you? Is that what you do?"

Wham. She's got me. That's not what I do. At least I don't think I do. I mean I can't even decide what I want with Zack and Bobby. And I am letting other people make the decision for me. I think that's what I'm doing. I really don't even know anymore. I go downstairs to wait for Bobby.

My parents are sitting at the kitchen table, working on their checkbook. That's always a good time to stay clear of them. I go into the living room to wait.

My stomach's in knots. I wonder what Zack's doing. I even wonder what Sandy's doing. I wonder why it's taking Bobby so long to get here. He's a half hour late. He used to do that all the time. I'd forgotten about that.

Finally I hear the horn honk. He's not even coming up to the door. He did that after we'd been going out for a while. I would have thought he'd come up to the door this time to show that things would be different. I guess he's pretty sure of himself.

I go out. He's sitting behind the wheel. I get in on the other side. He smiles at me. He's wearing a football varsity jacket.

"Hi," I say.

He keeps smiling and says, "Let's go for a soda and hamburger. We can talk there."

I nod.

Neither of us says much for most of the ride.

As we pull up into Stewart's, Bobby says, "I've missed you. I'm glad we're getting back together."

I shake my head. "I didn't say that we were. I just said we'd talk about it."

He says, "But I know we will. Remember all the

fun we used to have? You know you like hanging around with the high-school crowd. Being driven places. And you know I'm just crazy about you."

He pulls into a parking space, turns off the engine, and leans back, looking very sure of himself.

I take a good look at him. He's very attractive, tall, kind of strong-looking, the kind of guy that most of the kids who have been teasing me would love to go out with.

I say, "If you are so crazy about me, why'd you break up with me?"

He frowns. "I just got tired of your being such a scared kid about sex, and I knew Sandy wasn't."

I say, "Well, what makes you think I'm any different, that things will be different?"

He says, "Well, you're getting older, and I'm sure that you've got to be getting bored with that little kid you've been hanging around with."

He looks so sure of himself. I debate telling him that Zack turns me on more than he ever did, and that I really don't think he should be so sure of himself, that maybe he should go back to Sandy.

I don't say anything yet.

We order from the guy who comes out.

It is nice being able to go out with someone who has a driver's license. Zack won't have one for almost four years.

Bobby says, "There's a party at Marty's on Friday. I'll pick you up at eight."

For a second I'm tempted to say yes; then I realize there was no question.

"How can you assume I'm going with you?" I ask him. "You don't even ask, you just tell."

He says, "I know you want to go out with me again. Remember how upset you were when you found out about me and Sandy, when I told you it was over? And now I'm telling you I was wrong. Doesn't that make you happy?"

I wait until the guy bringing the order puts it on the window and leaves.

"Bobby, you're unbelievable. You walk out and then expect to come back as if nothing had ever happened."

He looks at me. "But I told you I'm sorry."

I look at him. He seems so sure of himself in his varsity jacket, with his driver's license, being seventeen. I think of Zack. He's smarter, nicer, more fun. I think of what I told Linda about doing what she wants to, not what others think she should do. Next I think of how the kids act to me in the hall. I don't even like them. Why do I have to worry about what they think of me? I wouldn't want them as friends anyway.

Bobby says, "Look, I'm giving you the chance to go out with me again. If you don't want to, just tell me. There are a lot of girls who would love the chance."

I almost laugh. When they handed out egos and conceit, Bobby must have gotten a double dose.

First I bite into my hamburger. Then I say, "I think maybe you should give one of them the pleasure of your company. I don't think I want to go out with you. In fact I know I don't."

He looks stunned. "But I thought . . . I mean, you were so upset when . . ."

"I was. But I'm not now. Look, Bobby, I don't think you know me anymore. You didn't even ask me what's new or anything. I don't want to be with someone who doesn't look at me and really see me."

"But I do."

"No." I realize it's true. "You don't, and you never did. Everything's always the way you want it."

He says, "Well, if that's the way you feel, there's no reason for us even to stay together any longer tonight." He turns on the engine.

"Don't you think you should honk so the guy gets the tray before you drive off?" I ask him.

He frowns. Bobby never likes to be told that he's goofed, considers it a sin. He honks. We drive back in silence.

When I get out of the car, I say, "It would have been nice if we could have ended up friends even without going out. But that's not possible because I don't think we've ever been friends."

He just frowns.

I go back into my house.

My parents are fighting over something in the checkbook. It sounds as if Mom wrote out a check to Melissa. I sneak past them. There's no way I'm getting involved in that.

Linda is still lying on her bed when I enter the room. "Everything OK?" she asks.

I nod and smile.

"No Bobby?"

"No Bobby."

"Good." She grins back. "Zack's a better audience for my jokes. And I like him better."

"Me too." I say.

I lie down on my bed to think about it. There are still going to be nasty remarks at school from some of the kids. My life's not going to drastically change. It hardly ever does when you're a kid. My parents certainly aren't going to change that much. It doesn't look like Melissa's going to be allowed to visit soon. I don't think I'm going to turn into a bio brain, like Erik Marks. I'm not even sure whether Zack and I will end up winning the pool, staying together for twenty-two years.

What I am sure of is that I finally did something for myself, that I'm learning to do what I think is best for me.

Maybe suing my parents for malpractice isn't as important as making sure that I don't do malpractice on myself. For the next newsletter, I'm going to write an article about that. I'll even sign it.

In the meantime, I'm calling Zack. We owe each other six and a half minutes.

DATE DUE